"We ain't takin' it anymore," the little man choked. "We can't eat right 'cause we pay you fer water, an' it don't rain an' there's no crops.—We can't even leave 'cause we owe you."

The crowd murmured angry agreement.

"We ain't gonna do it," the little man said doggedly. His face showed terror, but an even greater desperation. "If you're gonna keep it up—"

Phil saw the little man's hand tremble, and noticed for the first time that he wore an old Army gun stuck in the belt of his trousers. The wild look of his eyes told the rest. He was going to pull the gun.

Killian must have seen it too. His hand stole gentle across his chest, almost casually. Phil knew it was going for the Derringer.

He sprang forward and swung his fist hard into his face. The little man's head snapped back and he groaned, dropping the gun that had just cleared his belt. Phil spun around to face the nearest man.

It was utterly silent.

He saw the nearest man's eyes go from him to a point beyond him on the porch.

He looked back.

Killian's gun was in his hand. Behind him, Brewster and Grove held leveled revolvers.

The little man got to his knees. His mouth trickled a stream of bright red. He looked at Phil dazedly.

"You don't want to die," Phil muttered.

The little man rubbed his face, and a sob tore from his throat. "Don't make no diff'rence—can't live—"

Killian's voice crack

The men grumbled

Jove books by Jack M. Bickham

GUNMAN'S GAMBLE
HANGMAN'S TERRITORY

GUNMAN'S GAMBLE

JACK M. BICKHAM

J

JOVE BOOKS, NEW YORK

All characters in this book are
fictitious. Any resemblance to actual
persons, living or dead, is purely coincidental.

GUNMAN'S GAMBLE

A Berkley Book / published by arrangement with
the author

PRINTING HISTORY
Previously published by Ace Books, Inc.
Charter edition / April 1984
Jove edition / January 1989

For information address: The Berkley Publishing Group,
200 Madison Avenue, New York, New York 10016.

ISBN: 0-515-09998-8

Jove Books are published by The Berkley Publishing Group,
200 Madison Avenue, New York, New York 10016.

PRINTED IN THE UNITED STATES OF AMERICA

10 9 8 7 6 5 4 3 2 1

Chapter 1

THE SKY had already begun to streak with the pink and purple of nightfall when he rode into town, but the townsfolk came alive when they saw him.

He sat straight in the saddle, weariness etched in the sunburned lines of his face. Red dust coated his faded blue shirt and trousers, and his horse's head hung exhausted from a long ride. He wore a single gun low on his right hip. His saddle creaked in time with the slow thud of the horse's hooves as he rode down the narrow, dusty main street.

These things did not set him apart. He looked like a dozen other men who had ridden in the same day.

But on his right hand he wore a light yellow glove. That made him a gunman. Everyone looked twice.

A cow hand standing on the porch of the hotel saw the rider coming, stared hard, squinted into the dimness of the evening sky, and nudged a companion.

"Phil Patterson," he murmured.

The word spread.

Before the lone rider had progressed half the distance of the main street, most of the men in town knew who he was.

A farmer at the feed store heard the name, paled slightly, and hurried his wife and son into the wagon. He clucked at his horse and the wagon rumbled away from the store before the shopping was done.

The sheriff, a man of thirty-eight who had been in the town for fourteen years, nodded solemnly when told of the visit, and turned into his office. He closed the door and got busy looking over old circulars because he didn't want to be around if Phil Patterson started trouble.

Several cowboys in the bar moved to a back table where they'd be out of the way, and continued their card game. But they kept looking toward the door.

The clerk of the hotel, a mouse-like little man with a flowered vest and horn-rimmed spectacles, hurried up the stairs and to a room on the second floor. He tapped timidly on a door.

"Yes?" a man's voice answered.

"It's me," the clerk said in a whine.

The door opened.

The clerk said, "You were asking about Phil Patterson?—He just rode into town."

The young man in the doorway smiled, then smacked a fist into his palm. "I knew it," he said. "I knew I'd catch up with him!"

The one making all the commotion, Phil Patterson, knew precisely the effect he was having on the town. It was an old story, one he didn't particularly like, one he had come to expect and live with.

He rode to the livery stable and dismounted at the yawning doors. A boy hurried out and glanced up at him nervously.

"Yes sir?" the boy asked.

Phil handed him the reins. "Horse is tired. Put him up?"

The boy licked his lips. His frightened eyes shone in the twilight. "Yes sir, Mister Patterson. Yes sir!"

Phil smiled and handed the boy a coin. "Which way is the best hotel?"

"On'y one," the boy replied tautly. "Down to the corner."

Phil swung off his saddle bags and turned toward the corner. "I'll be back in the morning."

"Yes sir," the boy said, still awed.

Phil walked toward the corner, his stiff legs hurting numbly. He peeled the glove off his right hand and flexed the fingers slowly, getting full feeling into them. It was an automatic gesture, one that had saved his life.

He walked to the corner and turned it. The evening light slanted over the dusty, nearly deserted street. There had been two wagons in front of the store when he rode in, but they were gone now. Only the slow settling of dust showed the way they had gone. Horses still stood quiet at the hitching rack in front of the nearest saloon, and he heard the sound of men's voices within it. The voices were not loud or careless.

He had intended to go to the hotel first, and maybe buy a bath and clean up. But the town told him he had been recognized, and that meant he first had to go into the saloon. If any of them wanted him, he would be better off to go in at once and find it out.

His spurs clinked on the board sidewalk as he neared the saloon. He pushed the door open and stepped inside.

They hadn't lighted the lanterns yet, and it was dim. It smelled of sawdust and whiskey. A long bar at the left extended to the back of the room, where a few cowhands sat at a table playing cards. They all looked up when he entered. But they quickly looked down again, concentrating on their game.

He walked to the bar. The bartender, a hairy-armed man with a black mustache, looked up at him.

"Red eye," Phil said.

The bartender put a glass before him, and took a bottle from under the bar. He poured a drink and leaned back.

Phil gulped it. The hot liquid spread out in his empty stomach as he turned to lean against the edge of the bar and look around the room.

It was the old game, the one he had to play. He didn't bother anymore wishing that it could be different. This was the way it was, and it had long ago been too late to change anything. He had found that the killing was necessary less often if he acted like he was ready to do it.—Act like you felt, like you didn't ever want to have to kill anyone—and half the kids in town figured you had lost your nerve and called you out.

So the bravado. The quiet waiting, readiness.

He had another drink and waited. The whiskey slid through his veins, singing a soft relaxation, but he fought it.

Other man came into the saloon, eyed him covertly, and went to the tables, or well down the bar. No one said anything or bothered him.

The door opened again, and a little man in a flowery vest hurried in. He looked around nervously, saw Phil, swallowed, and started toward him.

Phil stood straighter, waiting.

"Mis—Mister Patterson?" the little man squeaked.

"Yes," Phil said softly.

The room had suddenly gotten still as a tomb.

"One of my—a man at the hotel," the little man stammered, his eyes wide with fright. "He said you —he said he'd—like to see you."

Phil looked at him. "Tell him to come over."

Beads of perspiration glistened on the man's forehead. "He said—would you please—come outside."

Phil put his glass down. He took a deep breath. "Where is he?"

"He's—the hotel—"

"Tell him to meet me in the street."

"No—he said—"

"Tell him to meet me in the street."

The clerk seemed to shrink before the steel in his voice. He turned and scurried out the door.

Phil turned to the bar. He had just begun to believe that his luck would hold, that he wouldn't have to meet anyone. A sick disgust turned over in his stomach. He fought it down. A cold resolution came up in its place.

You're a gunman, he thought. You'll never escape it.

He glanced steadily around the room and then started for the door.

As it closed behind him he heard chairs overturn as men ran to the window to see what would follow.

It would be a big show, he thought bitterly. Seeing a man die.

The street lay deserted in the last rays of daylight. The hotel stood gaunt and yellow at an angle across the street. The heat of the day clung to the dusty street, radiating at his parched skin and sweat-soaked shirt.

He loosened the gun in its holster and took a step into the street.

The door of the hotel burst open and a young man hurried across the porch and down the steps, not even looking up.

Phil stopped. This was his man. He frowned. He had never had one come at him this way before, carelessly, not even trying, not looking up to gauge the distance.

He let his legs spread slightly in the most comfortable stance.

The man came off the steps and looked up. He stopped dead.

Phil went into a crouch. His blood froze, time stopped and he stared at the man. All of existence —life—focusing down onto the outlines of his body.

The man took a hesitant step forward—then another.

Phil's right arm tensed.

The light caught the other man's face.

Phil's breath sucked in.

The man said huskily, "Phil?"

"Is it—Jonathon?" Phil muttered unbelievingly.

"Gawd yes!" the man cried.

Then Phil moved. He stumbled forward to meet the other man in the middle of the street. Their arms clasped around each other in a tight embrace.

"Man," Jonathon grinned, shoving Phil playfully into his hotel room. "I thought you was gonna bore me."

Phil shook his head, still trying to believe it. "I thought you were someone calling me out."

Jonathon carefully lit the lantern. Its yellow light made the gray evening of the window seem dark and far away. Phil looked around the flowered walls, then tested the softness of the bed.

"Been a while since I was in one of these," he said.

"Me too," Jonathon grinned. "I been here two days waitin' for you, though, an' I'm gettin' used to it."

Phil looked at his brother's sunburned face, remembering the crooked grin, the dancing hazel eyes, the yellow hair. It was the Jonathon he remembered, but a man now, able to take care of himself.

Then he realized what Jonathon had said.

"You've been waiting for me?" he asked.

"Sure!" Jonathon grinned.

"How did you know—?"

Jonathon ran his hands through his hair in a familiar gesture. "I been huntin' you. I just missed you at Abilene. They said you'd be headin' out through here. I figgered you'd haf to stop."

"You figured right," Phil admitted. Then—"But why?"

Jonathon lit a cigarette off the lantern. "You mean why tail you?"

"Of course."

"Well, Phil, you don't exactly pick up your mail regular, an' I had to find you as soon's I could."

With these words the boy's face grew suddenly sober, and Phil's insides moved with a twinge of pain.

"Maw?" he asked huskily.

Jonathon laughed. "Nope!—Nothin' like that—she's fine."

"Then what?" Phil asked, leaning forward. "There *is* something wrong."

Jonathon studied his cigarette. "You been gone from Redwater nine years, Phil."

"You don't have to tell me what I already know," Phil said. "Get to the point."

Jonathon met his gaze. "The point's that it's time you come home."

Phil leaned back on the bed. "You know better."

"No," Jonathon said. "I don't know no better. —We need you back there now an' I come to make you a proposition."

Phil stared at the ceiling. "I'll never go back to Redwater."

"Cripes sake!" Jonathon burst out. "Hear what I got to say!"

Phil sat up and looked at him.

"We got troubles in Redwater," Jonathon said. "We need help."

"I can't help you."

"Maybe you can't. I don't know.—You goin' north like they say to be a hired gun again?"

Anger flushed Phil's face. "Is it any of your business?"

Jonathon's hands—big, work-gnarled hands—twisted nervously. But he said doggedly, "I don't know if it is or ain't.—Are you?"

"I have a job waiting," Phil admitted.

"Killin'? That what you want to do?"

"It's a job," Phil said, not trying to hide the bitterness. "At least you don't have to sneak into a man's herd and kill a heifer and carry part of it off and eat it half raw because you're starving. You don't have to rob a bank or kill people you might like. It's a range war up there and everybody will be a hired gun. It'll be honest."

"It'll be murder," Jonathon said softly.

Phil met his gaze. "If somebody else said that, Jonathon—"

His brother didn't flinch. "I know. It don't make no difference. I gotta say it because we got troubles and you're the only guy we know can help."

Phil reached in his pocket for tobacco. He took a deep breath. "Let's just forget it," he said lightly. "Tell me how you've been doing on the farm. How's—how are everyone at home?"

"You mean Cassie, maybe?"

"I didn't mean Cassie," Phil lied. "I had forgotten Cassie."

Jonathon swung his booted feet up on the edge of the bed. "Cassie got married to Fred Grove coupla years ago. She's a widow now. Fred got stove in by a horse."

Phil looked at his hands.

He should have known she would get married, but somehow the idea had remained abstract. Even trying to forget her—and almost succeeding—he had never really visualized her as married.

And now a widow. It seemed odd that she should be a widow. He still remembered her as 17, fresh and so young and pretty she made your throat hurt dry when the sun caught in her hair and she laughed, making that tinkling sound in the air with her laughter.

With an effort he shut out the flood of memory. He said, "That life is all behind me now."

"It's been pretty rough back there," Jonathon said. "You ever wish you could come back, Phil?"

"It's too late," Phil rapped.

"It might not be," Jonathon insisted. "Not if you come back with me an' be our marshal."

Phil rocked back.

"I ain't kiddin' you," Jonathon added hastily. "A bunch of folks got together, secret, an' had me come huntin' for you to see."

"Me a marshal?" Phil asked incredulously.

"We need you," Jonathon said simply.

"You'd still have a marshal," Phil said bitterly, "if I hadn't been a coward."

Jonathon made a clucking sound of impatience. "Come on, Phil!"

Phil lit his cigarette. "Let's hear it," he said through the smoke. "We may as well go through all the motions. Then when I say no you'll know I mean it."

Jonathon licked his lips. "You know Cy Killian?"

Phil thought. "No," he said finally. "I know a Jack Killian. He's in California."

"It's Jack's brother."

"In Redwater?"

"Yeah. He's plumb took the place over."

"How?"

"He brought some stuff—the hotel an' a saloon an' stuff, an' then he got about a half a dozen guys workin' for 'im. He's got a dam acrost the crik. He's sellin' water. He's rustlin' cows an' buildin' him a herd."

Phil shifted his weight so his gun wasn't underneath him. "And you want me to kill Killian. Is that it?"

"We don't want to hire you jus' for a gun," Jonathon snapped. "Will you gimme a chanct?"

Phil kept quiet.

"He's got a canyon in the mountains someplace," Jonathon said. "He takes the cows an' gets 'em in there, an' we don't know where. If we could find out where he takes the cows, maybe, we could prob'ly handle the rest our own selves."

Phil saw it all at once. "You want me to join his bunch and then double cross him. Is that it?"

Jonathon flushed. "Well, somethin' like that."

"I almost wish you'd wanted me as a hired gun," Phil clipped. "It wouldn't have made me feel very good, thinking my own brother thought of me as a gun, but at least it would have been a job."

Jonathan's eyes widened. "You figger it'd be too dirty, doublecrossin' 'im?"

Phil drew on his cigarette. "Something like that. Skip it."

"We got up five hundred dollars," Jonathon said softly. "We'll pay you as soon's you do it. You can do it any way you want, only jus' stop 'em from wreckin' Redwater."

"For what?" Phil asked. "So I can leave again as soon as I've taken care of your dirty work? Those people in Redwater hate my guts. I don't blame them."

"You could stay after it was over with," Jonathon said. "You an' me—we could get some cows—"

"I can't put up my gun," Phil muttered. "I can't stop till somebody beats me. Then I'll be dead."

"Is that the way you want it?" Jonathon snapped back, suddenly angry. "You like the killin'—"

Phil reached forward and grabbed the front of his shirt. The shirt tore as he jerked hard, so that their faces were an inch apart.

"Don't ever say that!" he hissed. "Just shut it up!"

Jonathon's face hardly changed. His lips compressed and green anger danced in his eyes.

Phil stared into his eyes, seeing his brother. He let go.

"I'm sorry," he said huskily.

Jonathon stood without emotion. "Guess I'll be goin'."

"Where?" Phil asked.

"Home. If you ain't goin', I'll haf to get back because that leaves me."

Phil frowned. "You mean to go after this Killian and his gang?"

Jonathon sighed. "You figger I'll just go back and sit on my fanny?"

Phil stood and took his arm. "Is this another trick to get me to go with you?"

"Hell no!" Jonathon flamed. "I come after you because I figgered, 'Well, this is the chanct for Phil to come back an' help us an' get hisself straightened out.' But if you don't want to, I'll go back an' see what I can do."

"Is Killian a gunman?" Phil asked soberly.

Jonathon shrugged. "He a greaser. He's fairly fast. He's got a guy workin' for him, Jack Brewster—"

"Brewster?" Phil interrupted sharply.

"Yeah. He's a real good 'un with a gun, but—"

"I saw him once. He's plenty good. You can't face him. Brewster will kill you."

Jonathon smiled lazily. "Maybe if I go back an' try, then some of the others'll finish the job."

"Okay," Phil said disgustedly, angry without any reason he could recognize. "Okay!—Don't expect to trick me into going back. Go on back and get yourself killed, if you want to be a big hero in a little red puddle in the street. If—"

He stopped. His brother suddenly blinked, and his eyes got wet. Jonathon had started all at once to cry.

"Oh hell," Phil muttered.

Jonathon didn't make a sound. He just stared, blinking, tears filling his eyes.

Shocked and left defenseless, Phil turned away. If it had been someone else, he could have sneered. But knowing how to sneer didn't help when it was Jonathon.

It showed it was the same Jonathon, a man now, but the same kid underneath: the same kid he had known as his brother in Redwater.

"Oh quit," he rasped. "I don't care what you do."

Jonathan sniffed and pulled out a red hankie. He wiped his face.

"I come here because I thought you might help," he said, muffled. "I thought—well—I thought maybe if it worked out we could be together—I got me a girl, an' I thought maybe me and Thelma—and you an' Cassie—we could homestead or somethin'—"

"My God," Phil groaned. "You're a kid in a man's body!—I can't go back there!—Do you think they really want me to?"

"They said so," Jonathon said slowly.

Phil took his brother's arm. "Listen! Why don't you just come up north with me? They've got jobs riding where you don't have to use a gun if you don't want to.—I could get it fixed so we could ride together. We—"

Jonathon shook his head. "Momma's down there, Phil. So's my girl. I tol' you."

"Couldn't you?" Phil asked softly, as if sensing that it was a moment of weakness.

Phil rolled another cigarette. "Does Killian have all good men like Brewster?"

"They're pretty good," Jonathon said. "Not as good as you."

Something in his voice made Phil look at him. He was grinning from ear to ear.

"I'm not going," Phil snapped.

Jonathon laughed. "You're going!—By Gawd, Phil, you're going! I can tell the way you look!"

"No," Phil said.

"We can leave in the mornin'," Jonathon said. "It's a heck of a long ride."

Chapter 2

PHIL PATTERSON had become a gunman—a killer—without really willing it. There had been those who thought he liked guns too much, practiced and hunted with too much intensity of purpose for a boy, but he hadn't ever intended to be a killer. It had just happened.

Redwater was a small North Texas town, and nothing much ever happened there. Phil's father had died when Phil was ten and Jonathon was eight, and Phil had been head of a household—a farmer made wiry and tough by hard work—six years when the town's first real excitement in a long time made him a killer, a coward, then a gunman. It had happened quickly. . . .

He had known something was wrong the moment Cassie rode up to the house, her gray riding pants heavy with red dust, her dark hair flying as she dismounted in a leap and ran toward the porch where he sat shelling peas.

"What's going on?" he called to her.

She came onto the porch, a slim girl his own age, lovely and tanned and strong. Her fine features showed worry-lines and anxiety.

"Our horses," she said.

"What about them?" he asked.

"Somebody," she said. Then she shook her head and started again. "They've been stolen."

Phil stood slowly. "Not your string!"

She nodded, meeting his eyes. "Daddy and Lester have started after them."

Phil felt dull anger and resentment tug at his insides. Cassie's father, Jake Michaels, raised the best horses in the country. Cassie's own string wasn't the kind a cowboy would want for hard work, but they were the kind that would gladden any man's eye. Fine-tuned, speedy little thoroughbreds, perfectly groomed and gentle, without the gut-tearing, ground-eating gait of work horses. Phil knew how much work and money they had cost to breed and raise, and he knew how much Cassie loved them.

"Who stole them?" he asked.

"We don't know," she said, fighting tears. "They didn't leave much—daddy left the first thing, awfully mad—"

"They didn't try to go cross country on your horses," Phil said.

"No. They led them. Daddy said they'll sell them."

Phil stepped through the door of the house and reached out to a nail where his gun belt hung. He swung it out and strapped it around his waist.

"I didn't come to ask you to go," Cassie said quickly. "You'd better stay here."

"I can take care of myself," Phil muttered, excitement pumping into his veins.

"I know you can," she said. "But Jonathon and your mother. . ."

"Jonathon's fourteen. He can handle things here. And nobody bothers us sodbusters anyway."

If the bitterness crept into his voice as he said it,

he didn't try to hide it. Before his father's death the little house on Hog Creek had been a good place, nothing fancy, but a place where there were visitors and friends and the rich smell of tobacco in the evenings. Before the accident there had been cattle to run, and hired help.

And it had been nearly the same for a while after pop died. People rode by frequently, brought supplies, and helped do chores. Some of the men even did the work of taking the cattle to market free, because Phil's mother needed the money that first winter.

But people forgot, and Phil had to take over by himself. There was no herd for income, and no money in the bank. Phil and Jonathon raised corn and okra and squash, and some peanuts to sell in town. They hunted too, both of them. They got along somehow after people stopped coming by very often.

No one had stopped being kind or good. They had just forgotten.

All but Jake Michaels. He didn't forget. He didn't offer charity because it would have been refused, but he always seemed to have some odd job to be done when things were roughest. And he took Phil and Jonathon in the canyon sometimes, along with his own son, Lester, and set up cans for them to shoot at. He showed them how to draw a gun and fire it from the hip, and laughed and encouraged Phil when he showed a natural talent for it. He was the sheriff. Phil idolized him.

And Cassie—well, that had been natural for so long that they might have taken it for granted if their emotions had not run so deep. They would get married pretty soon—as soon as Jonathon got a couple years older and could take care of things, and then the two families would be one.

Now, as Phil saddled his horse—a horse Michaels had sold him—to go help chase the men who had stolen Cassie's string, he thought how it was right for him to go and help.

Cassie, standing beside him, said,"You'll be careful, Phil."

The soft way she said it made him look at her.

"Sure," he said hesitantly. "—What's the matter?"

She had to squint into bright sunlight to look into his face. "This isn't just an excuse to see how well you can use that gun."

He swallowed. He didn't feel anger. "No," he said. "I won't use it unless I have to."

She touched his arm. "Daddy says you're so good—he says if you ever get started you might not be able to stop because you're so good."

He grinned. "Don't worry about that. I've practiced a lot, sure. But that's just been for fun. —I don't guess I'll even know what to do if we actually have trouble."

Then he swung onto his horse and rode away.

He caught up with Jake and his son, Lester, near Elm Fork. It was nearly nightfall. They had made dry camp under a group of stunted cottonwoods.

Michaels, a bulky man in gray pants, turned so that the faint light touched the dull star on his vest. He didn't look surprised.

"Thought you'd be along," he grunted.

"Have you seen them yet?" Phil asked quickly.

"Not yet," Michaels snorted. "They're making time."

Phil loosened his saddle and swung it to the ground. "Know who they are yet?"

"No," Lester said in a tight voice. "But we will."

Phil looked at the younger man. Lester was his own age, and the old temper was showing. It seemed funny for Lester to be so totally unlike his father in temperament; they looked so much alike —both so blond they looked almost like albinos, both stubble-bearded, squatly built, and powerful. They were a pair, with their mild-looking blue eyes that showed anger so quickly, their faded work clothes, their thick wrists and supple hands.

But the older man showed none of the impatience that made Lester jumpy. His clear eyes did not smile, but they showed no heat, and his movements were leisurely as he cut slabs of dried bacon and broke biscuits.

Michaels looked up at Phil. "Figure we won't haf to chase 'em too far. Imagine they'll be holed up at Bluffton."

Phil had slipped hobbles on his horse's legs. He looked around at the grass.

"He won't go off far," Michaels said easily. "Grass is good."

Phil squatted beside the tiny fire.

"How'd you find out?" Michaels asked.

"Cassie told me."

"Figures."

Lester stood restlessly, walked around, then squatted again. "You hear all about it, Phil?"

"I don't know," Phil said.

"It was the Shed bunch," Lester blurted.

Electricity tingled through Phil's body. "Are you sure?"

"No," Michaels said. "He ain't sure."

"Who else'd think they could get away with it?" Lester snapped hotly.

Michaels stirred the fire. "Dunno. Maybe you're right."

Phil stared into the flames. It made sense, Lester's theory that it was the Sheds. Especially if they were heading for Bluffton. It was easy to change brands and sell stolen horses and defy the owner to prove the crime if you practically owned a town, as the Sheds practically owned Bluffton. There were stories about men whose horses had been stolen by the Sheds, men who went after what belonged to them and never came back.

"If it is them," Phil said, "what do you do?"

Michaels shrugged. He didn't look up. "I want my stuff."

After they ate, Michaels took out his big blue gun and rubbed it with an oiled rag. He rubbed the holster, too, and spun the gun in his hand several times. Then he got up and walked into the night, and in a moment Phil heard the leather-slapping sound of Michaels practicing his draw.

That told Phil there wouldn't be just a fight. There would be death.

They rode into Bluffton late the next afternoon. They had been able to see it for ten miles because there wasn't a tree anywhere. It was a dog-eared little town, maybe a dozen wooden buildings, most of them closed. It was a dying place, for the creek had been dry for three summers, and even the scraggly bushes were brown and beaten. It was a stopping point, a place with one deep water well. The cattlemen and farmers had left it. So had most of the shopkeepers, gamblers and hangers-on. It was almost a ghost town now, a town run by the Sheds.

Michaels rode in the middle, with Phil on his left and Lester on his right. As they approached the town Michaels motioned for them to spread out slightly. It was still and hot, and flies buzzed on their horses' backs.

"What are we slowing up and spreading out for?" Lester asked huskily. "The Sheds' place is a couple miles the other side of town. In the gully."

Michaels rubbed sweat from his face. "Didn't you see the guy ride out when we were still a couple miles off?"

Lester looked at his father, then at Phil. "Did you see him, Phil?"

"Yes," Phil admitted. "He went out the back way, trying to keep the town buildings between us and him."

Michaels smiled grimly. "You saw the dust."

"It had to be a rider," Phil said. "Going fast."

Michaels nodded. "So we won't have to go out there. They'll come to us."

They rode into the town. An old man, his chair tilted back against the weathered front of the beat-up general store, watched them ride by without showing any sign of recognition. The sun beat down fiercely on the unprotected buildings, and it was as silent as was the range. The clopping of their horses' hooves was the only sound.

Following Michaels' lead, they rode to the big blackened barn in the middle of the town.

Beside the yawning front doors was a crudely painted sign. They got down to read it.

HORS SALE SHEDS TODAY
COM WAN COME ALL

"The lousy bastards!" Lester cried harshly.

"I guess we've come to the righ place," Michaels said evenly.

Lester stepped up to the sign and ripped it from the wall.

"That's not going to—" Michaels began. Then he stopped.

Phil looked in the direction of his gaze.

Five riders.

Already they were close enough to be seen clearly in outline. Two of the horses, the way they stepped daintily, were obviously Cassie's. One looked like her favorite.

"Of all the guts," Lester muttered thickly.

Michaels didn't say anything, but he moved to the side a bit, lining himself up so his back was to the barn. Very casually he touched the butt of his gun, loosening it in the holster.

With a chill of anticipation, Phil did likewise, getting on his right and six paces away.

"I'll talk," Michaels said softly.

The men slowed their mounts as they neared the edge of town, coming straight down the narrow, dusty street toward them.

Phil looked to his side to make sure he had room. He did not feel afraid. His nerves tingled vibrantly alert. He was thinking of Lester who was slow with guns. Lester had practiced, but not as he had. Michaels had once told Phil that Lester was not fast enough. "He's a newer kind," Michaels had said a trifle sadly. "Maybe it's better. If you're not fast, nobody'll ever want to try you."

Phil knew he was fast, but he had never been tried. Now the riders walked their horses nearer, and he felt prickling excitement. This would be his test. He hadn't realized before that he wanted a test, but he saw now that he did. He wanted this fight badly.

He realized with a shock that it had very little, if anything, to do with Cassie's horses or a debt to Michaels. It was curiosity. He had to know if they could throw a gun fater than he could. He didn't think so. He wanted to know. He had to know.

The men came within gunshot, into the long, slanting shadow of the barn, and Phil looked at each of them.

His eyes skipped over four of them—a tall one with a red shirt, a little man with pockmarks all over his face, the squatty older one who had a rifle in a scabbard on the saddle, the one in blue shirt and pants whose left arm looked withered.

It was the fifth one he wanted. Seeing everything at once he knew it instantly.

The man was on the far end, nearer Lester. He sat round-shouldered in the saddle, and he couldn't have been over five feet, six. His bulky chest and shoulders strained at the faded orange-colored shirt he wore. His hat, pulled down low, didn't hide a stubble red beard and a wide mouth that had been stained by tobacco.

His thick, hairy arms seemed too long for his body. He sat the saddle loosely, his right hand dangling lax near the bottom of a plain black leather holster. His single gun was tied down, and it had a pearl handle. It had been well used.

Phil's eyes took in even the missing button on his shirt, the grass stain on the knees of his trousers, his muddy boots—brown mud from the river bottom—the frayed strands of his bandana, the sweat stains under his arms.

Something along the back of Phil's neck told him; here is the best of them. Here is the one who can kill you.

The men stopped not ten feet away. Saddle leather creaked, but they didn't make any motion to get down.

Phil's eyes flicked over the others, then back to the red-haired one. With a tiny shock he met the man's eyes.

They watched him intently, without emotion.

Phil's blood went icy. They had found each other.

The man in the middle, the one with the withered arm, spoke in a croaking-dry voice:

"Come a fur piece?"

"Redwater," Michaels said.

The man picked his nose. "Fur piece, aw right."

For a moment no one said anything. The horses stamped.

"Yuh take our sign down?" the man asked mildly.

"The horses you're selling belong to us," Michaels said.

None of them made any sign at all. The one with the withered arm looked at his fellows. "Hear thet? —Yuh know anythin' 'bout horses bein' stole?"

Again Phil's eyes met those of the red-haired man. He couldn't see any emotion there at all. It was like looking into the windows of a vacant house. A rill of sweat went down his back.

But his calm detached him almost entirely from the setting. It was just the two of them, really, and they both knew it. In a moment, surely, they would know which was best with his gun. For the loser there would be death.

Michaels said clearly, "We took the sign down, and now we want our animals."

"Yuh," the man replied coolly, "don't get nothin'."

"We're taking them," Michaels said.

The man leaned over the pommel of his saddle. He smiled. "Wal, mister, ah guess yuh better ride afore we get mad."

Silence. The blood beat a crescendo in Phil's brain. The blurred edges of his vision took in all of them, straining for that first movement, and no one had moved yet. The red-haired one had never taken his eyes away from him. Lester was closer. But Lester didn't know. Maybe even Michaels didn't know.

Take the red-haired one—*know*—then if Lester missed, if Michaels couldn't get the second man—

Red Hair's expression didn't change at all. But his hand blurred.

Phil's hand shot to his holster and the gun came out. The other's gun cleared leather and started up. Phil's thumb hit the hammer of his gun and it slammed back against his hand, shattering the silence with smoke and recoil.

Red Hair's face suddenly fell. He looked surprised, baffled, hurt. A great crimson splotch showed suddenly on the front of his shirt. His gun fell. He started out of the saddle.

Michaels had drawn at the same instant. But Phil knew racingly that Michaels had been slower, had whirled his gun on another of the men as his own bullet went home. Michaels' gun went off twice and the man in the middle spun backward. Lester's gun splattered with no apparent effect. Phil swung his arm and fired into the orange flame of another's shot. Something zipped past his ear and the man grunted and slid to the side. Phil's ears roared and went deaf in the instant of deafening gunfire. He saw Michaels' gun go off, and a man's face caved in in a sickening mess. Dust flew up beneath the hooves of rearing horses. Two of the men wheeled their mounts.

One of the men raised his gun as his horses spun to charge away. The gun swung toward Phil. Phil shot from the hip. The man hurtled off the horse as if he had been hit with a sledge-hammer. In the instant Phil watched him fall the other man dug his spurs to his horse and raced down the street.

Lester cursed shrilly and banged away—twice, three times—after the fleeting figure. "Damn 'em!" he cried angrily. "Let's go get that one!"

Suddenly the dust hung heavy in silent air. Smoke curled from Phil's hot gun and the palm of his hand stung from its recoil. The horses had broken and scattered. Two of them were not in sight. One stood nervously fifty paces away, watching them. Another, a roan, pranced in the main street, tossing his head with fright and anger.

At Phil's feet lay a dead man, a hamburger-faced corpse killed by Michaels. Ten feet away, the man Phil had last killed lay face down, twitching in death. Another was balled up at the door of the barn; he moaned harshly, holding a gaping wound in his stomach. The red-haired one lay flat on his back, arms outstretched as if thrown out to cushion the impact of fall. The front of his shirt was brownish red. He didn't move. The wind caught his hat and twirled it over and over on the rim until it hit the side of the barn and flopped still.

Phil looked at Michaels. Michaels' eyes slitted in grim understanding.

Temples pounding, Phil walked to the body of the red-haired one. He looked down into the face.

The egg-white eyes stared back at him with the stark ugliness of death. The man's lips were drawn back from yellow teeth, but not in anger. He looked surprised, like maybe a kid who got an unexpected birthday present. His hand was still shaped in the claw that had been on his gun when he died. Bright blood still welled like a fountain from his chest.

Phil turned and staggered to the door of the barn. He put out a hand unsteadily and leaned against the rough black wood.

His stomach heaved. He bent over in a violent fit and saw his vomit hit the earth and roll in dust balls around his feet. His vision blurred and he gasped for breath, and the instant he got it into his lungs he threw up again, even more violently. Nothing came up and he retched again. Bent double, he fought through the paroxysm.

Then a hand touched his shoulder. With a shuddering effort he swallowed and clenched his teeth against the rotten-tasting bile that surged up in his throat.

He wiped his eyes with his sleeve and looked at Michaels through watery eyes. Beyond Michaels he saw Lester, watching in amazement.

"I was watching him too," Michaels said softly.

"He—he was the best," Phil choked.

"Him and me," Michaels said musingly, "would've been real close."

Phil met his eyes, and something hot and proud surged up inside him. "I beat him bad."

Michaels smiled, but his eyes looked sad. "You got him in the heart, looks like.—Right in the heart."

Michaels' keen eyes held a new look. Phil felt with a chill that it was a man-to-man look, one tempered with a great deal of respect.

"You got the other one in the chest too," Michaels said, turning to look at the wild scene.

"You got him in almost exactly the same place. I thought I was pretty good. I missed once, and one of them is gut-shot. I thought Lester was fairly good. He never hit anybody."

Phil stared at the older man, frozen by the toneless sound of his voice.

Michaels said, "You're good, Phil. You might be too good, I don't know."

Chapter 3

JONATHON'S arrival and offer of 500 dollars to go back to Redwater made Phil remember his start as a gunman—his first realization that he was really good with a gun. It made him remember the rest of it, too, the way he had tried to turn back after it was too late, and how it had resulted in disaster.

Michaels had had more than intuition to tell him that the red-haired man was the most dangerous. On the way back home—they rode fast with the four animals they had recovered—he told Phil that the red-haired one had been Duane Harper.

Harper had been the Shed gang's number one gun. Phil had heard of him for years, and knew of his reputation as one of the fastest men in Texas. The knowledge that he had killed him left him with an odd mixture of emotions, half hot, crazy pride, half sick worry.

Michaels seemed to understand both.

"You've been going the way to being a gun fighter since you were ten," he said on the trail home. "Now you're just about there, and you're glad in one way, but you don't know if you really want to be one or not now that the choice is here. You better make up your mind fast."

"I'm not a gun fighter," Phil protested. "I don't want to be."

"I know," Michaels snapped, anger showing in the edge of his voice. "I know how you feel. You're like me. Like I was."

"But I'm no gun-slinger," Phil protested weakly.

"You had to *know* back there," Michaels said. "You didn't throw down on Harper because he looked dangerous or because you were worried about the horses. You did it because you knew he was good, and you didn't know about yourself."

"Maybe I did," Phil admitted doggedly, his nerves jerking. "Maybe I did want to know.—But now I do. I can—"

"You can wait till the next time," Michaels said bitterly. "Even if you didn't have to know again, there's always someone that has to try *you.* If you're not the kind that goes looking they'll hunt you."

"I'll quit right now," Phil said, dry-throated. "I'm through."

"Maybe you are and maybe you aren't," Michaels said darkly. "I heard Harper was good enough that Wes Hardin was huntin' for him. If Hardin or anybody else hears about you beating Harper, they'll just have to come see you."

"I won't wear my gun anymore," Phil vowed softly, seeing the whole stretch of events that could ruin him. He took a deep breath and felt sick again. "Honest to God, Mister Michaels! I don't want it! I'm through!"

"I don't know if you *can* be through," Michaels said. "There was a time when maybe *I'd* of had to try you. I grew out of it. But some guys don't. It doesn't have to do with the killing. It's just the *knowing.*"

"I don't want any of it," Phil breathed fervently. "Isn't there some way I can get out of it?"

Michaels shrugged. "Word'll get out. The one that saw it and got away. Maybe some of 'em will come to Redwater."

"If they do," Phil said huskily, "I got to fight 'em."

"You don't," Michaels said sharply. "You can stay home with no gun on. I can handle them. If you really want me to."

"I do. I don't want it. I just want to stay here in Redwater and do a job. I don't want any more."

Michaels studied him gravely. "All right. We'll get back soon. I want you to stay home. Let Jonathon do the coming to town. You stay home. No guns. If anybody comes to town asking after you, I'll handle it."

"But that'd be fighting my battles."

"It's that, or you becoming a gun-slinger.—Which will it be?"

Phil groaned. He didn't have to answer.

"All right then," Michaels said. "You stay home, even if they come to town looking.—Promise?"

"Okay," Phil said weakly. "I—I promise."

When they got back to Redwater, Phil saw Cassie, and they went into the garden. He told her what had happened. At first she shuddered and said nothing, and a honey bee buzzed in the silence and Phil brushed the insect away.

"It was a fair fight," he told her haltingly. "There was five of them, and just us three. Harper went for his gun first. I beat him. He was on his horse. Maybe that was why I beat him. I beat him bad."

Still Cassie did not speak, her face averted from

him, the hot sun bright on her dark hair. He wondered racingly why he had had to say he beat Harper bad. The pride—the rotten pride. The gunman in him had made him say it, and he hated it. He had almost told her how he had shot both men in the heart.

"What now?" she asked finally, without any tone at all.

"I don't know," he said. "I'll put my gun up. Your dad says he'll take care of it if anybody comes looking for me."

She didn't say anything and he looked at her, turning her face gently with his hand. He saw tears on her cheeks.

"Honey!" he cried.

"Will you really stay out of it?" she asked huskily.

"Yes!—I'll stay out of it and—"

"Will you *really?*" she demanded fiercely. "Or will you go out again?"

"No," he said quickly. "I'm putting my gun up, Cassie. I'm—"

"Will you practice any more?" She pointed toward the river bottom. "Will you go down there—every afternoon—and shoot a box of shells at pieces of paper and things I can't even see, and come back with your hand all red and sore from hitting that—that *gun* as you draw it?"

The scorn and fear in her voice made him shrink. "No," he said. "No, I won't. Maybe I ought to—well—just keep my hand limber. I mean—you might meet up with a snake, or something, and you ought to be able to defend yourself. . . ."

"Oh Phil!" Her voice broke. "Is it something born into you? Can't you see what's going to happen?"

"It *won't* happen!" he pleaded. "I won't let it!"

She fixed him with her lovely, angry eyes. "If you love me," she said in a trembling tone, "you'll remember."

"I will," he said. "So help me God."

And so he had promised two of the people he loved most. And he was scared.

The next morning when he went into the garden with Jonathon and started harvesting their peanuts, he didn't wear his glove as he usually did. Jonathon asked him about it and got a curt answer. The sun advanced in the bronze sky, and sweat trickled through dust-ruts down his aching body, and he worked all the harder so he wouldn't think about anything else. The peanuts came out, great clumps of roots and globules in the dusty soil. He forced himself to use his right hand, the one that had always been protected. The soft skin rubbed on the rough plants, and blistered, and tore. Then the hand started to bleed, and he kept right on working.

But the work didn't soothe the dark dread in his guts, and he knew what it meant when Lester rode up to the front gate that evening.

Lester's face shone white in the evening dimness. He piled off his lathered horse and leaned panting against the fence.

"Four of 'em," he gasped. "Lookin' for you. Pop's gonna meet 'em."

"Alone?" Phil rapped. "Four of them and he's going against them alone? Did he send you for me?"

Lester shook his head wildly. "No—no, he'd whack me if he knew. But they're tough uns. Pop shut up Pederson before he could tell 'em where you live at, an' now he's gonna meet 'em by himself."

Phil's mind raced. He had promised not to go. If he went, he'd be breaking his word to Michaels and Cassie both. It would be the end, He would be a gunman from then on. But if he didn't go—and Michaels was killed—

"You gotta come help!" Lester pleaded. "Let's go!"

Phil looked down at his hand, the raw one he had punished all day.

"My God!" Lester grabbed him by the wrist. "Wha'd you *do?"*

Phil motioned numbly. "The peanuts—"

"You didn't wear your glove?"

"No—your dad said I had to stop . . . he knew this might happen."

"Well it has, and they'll kill him if you don't hurry."

Phil clenched the reddened gun hand, feeling the sparkling pain go into his wrist and elbow. He wanted to go. He had to. Michaels might die. But Michaels had said to stay home. Michaels wanted it that way. Michaels had once been the fastest gun in North Texas. He was smart. He thought like a winner. But maybe it wouldn't work out. Maybe Michaels would die and it would be his fault.

But maybe he would go to town, and Michaels could have done it alone, and then he'd be a killer, a gun-slinger, and he'd have to leave, and there would be more and more until somebody killed him.

Lester grabbed him by the arm. "Come on, Phil! Pop'll be going out there!"

Torn, Phil held back. "He said to stay out of it."

Lester's eyes gleamed with impotent tears. "He'll *die!"*

Phil turned toward the house, where his gun belt hung on a peg just inside the front door. He could go to town and help Michaels, and meet these big professional killers, and they could just see who was the best. They could really know who could sling a gun the fastest, who was the best man.

He recoiled with a choking oath. Even now he wasn't thinking of Michaels! Not really. It was the curiosity—the damned and damning need to know, the wondering whether it would be him still standing, or the other man, watching him die in the street.

"Are you coming?" Lester cried.

Phil looked at him through the pink haze of chaos. "Lester—"

Hatred suddenly drew Lester's mouth into an ugly line. He turned and vaulted onto his trembling horse. "I'll go," he clipped. "I'll go and help, and if you're a man, you'll go too."

Phil's insides shook with the longing to run for his horse. But he couldn't. If he went this time, there would be another time, and another, and then there would be leaving here in disgrace—no Cassie and no farm and no Jonathon, nothing, just the gun and the killing and the sickness.

"Phil!" Lester cried.

Phil shuddered with the effort. "I can't," he choked. "I—"

With a bitter curse, Lester spurred his horse away.

Phil stood at the front gate a long time, suspended from time, waiting. He felt nothing. Then, finally, he heard hoof-beats. He waited, sick.

It wasn't Lester. It wasn't Michaels. It was one

of the boys from town, a kid named Icly. His acne-scarred face gleamed with excitement in the darkness.

"Phil Patterson?" he called.

"Yes," Phil muttered woodenly.

"Some guys in town," the kid said lazily, enjoying it. "They said you come in or they come out."

Phil's hand smashed against the fence post, tearing flesh from his knuckles.

"They shot ole Michaels," the drawling voice said. "They shot ole Lester too. He ain't dead. He might could be though. They said now you come in or they come out."

Phil's eyes steamed hot. In the instant before he moved, he saw again the trips hunting with Michaels, the shooting lessons, the rides together, the talks, even the last trip together, the advice and the look in Michaels' eyes.

They had killed him.

The kid's voice said, "I said, they told me you should come in."

Phil looked at the kid, a hazy outline in the dimness, and he trembled with rage. Michaels was dead, and still they hadn't had enough. They had to have *him*. They had come for him, and Michaels had tried to right it. And now Cassie had no father, and Lester maybe was dead, and Jonathon and his mother had no one either, because it was all over and Phil Patterson was a gunman.

"You tell them," he said, his voice shaking, "that I'm coming in."

He strode into the house and grabbed the heavy gunbelt. He stopped at the water bucket on his way to the barn and plunged his raw hand into the cool water. Then he went into the barn and threw his saddle on his horse—the horse Michaels had provided him.

"Phil?" Jonathon's voice asked hesitantly from the shadows.

Phil jerked the cinch tight on the saddle.

"You goin' to town?" Jonathon asked softly, scared.

Phil flipped the holster strings around his leg and tied the gun down tight. He took the gun out carefully. He opened it and ejected two spent shells. He put in two clean, oily bullets and closed the gun. He held it in his raw hand. It felt good. It felt hot and heavy and solid.

He looked at Jonathon. "I won't be back," he said.

"Aw," Jonathon said weakly. "You'll—"

"I'll kill them," Phil said without feeling. Then I can't come back. Do you understand?"

Jonathon nodded soberly. "We'll—we'll do just fine, Phil."

Phil looked at him.

Then his emotions broke and he grabbed Jonathon in his arms.

"Take care of Mom," he muttered thickly. "Take care of yourself. I'll—maybe one day—"

Jonathon nodded, a frail boy fighting to be a man. He sniffled and wiped his nose on his shirtsleeve. "Don't you worry none, Phil."

Phil stepped back from him. He turned and mounted his horse.

He rode into town and found three of the men, and met them in the street, in almost total blackness.

He shot three times.

He walked around the town, silent and ashen-faced, asking for the fourth man. The fourth man had disappeared.

Phil mounted his horse again and pulled a thin yellow glove onto his right hand. He rode out of Redwater.

He had become a gun-slinger.

Chapter 4

NOW THE hot dryness of the autumn sun punished Phil and Jonathon as they rode south, toward Redwater again. The rolling hills, purple in the distance, wavered in the hot sunlight. The only sounds were the sighing of the vacant prairie wind and the soft clop of horses' hooves. Phil turned in the saddle to let the slight breeze hit his sweat-soaked back.

He still didn't know exactly why he was going back. But for whatever reason, he was going back. Maybe to die. But that didn't make much difference. It was the going back that counted. The *doing* something.

"Hey," Jonathon grinned suddenly. "You haven't said anything for a couple hours."

Phil smiled. "Meditating, or something."

"You all talked out already? I got lots more to tell, man."

"You've said plenty," Phil said. "What I'd like to know is where they take the cattle they run off."

"Nobody's ever seen 'em run any off," Jonathon said cautiously. "It's mostly mavericks."

"But you know they're being taken."

"Yeah. But there must be a hunderd dead end canyons in those mountains. They could be drivin' 'em into almost any one of 'em."

"It's some operation, selling water, rustling cows, running the Golden Eagle," Phil said. "So the thing to do is join the gang."

"I thought you wouldn't do that," Jonathon blurted.

"I have to," Phil said.

"I better tell you more about the guys, then."

"I know enough."

"You can't, Phil. I haven't told you that much."

Phil smiled grimly. "Cy Killian runs it. He looks like Jack, which means he's tall, heavy-set, dark. Maybe a breed or a greaser. He doesn't act like either. Smooth talker. Wears a Derringer under his left arm. He wears a coat to hide the gun.

"Jack Brewster," Phil went on, reciting, "is his number one man. He's built like you, only smaller. Five-seven or so, weighs maybe a hundred-fifty. He doesn't look like much, wears his gun high, has abnormally big hands that help. Hired gun. Fast. Likes shooting people.

"Dick Baxon. He's fairly good, loud clothes, left-handed, not really a gun-slinger. Smart. Arrogant. Eighteen, maybe twenty. Good with a rifle. Best horseman of the bunch. Gets the dirty jobs, like when a sodbuster starts giving them trouble and needs to be shot in the back."

He rolled a cigarette, then went on. "Pop Schwartz is the bushwacker. Old, white hair, potbelly, got shot in the throat once, so he talks in a whisper. He's been in half the gangs in the country. Knows everybody, nobody likes him.

"Tub—you didn't give me any other name. I never heard of him before. Probably a local one. Couldn't get his gun out in thirty minutes, but he's a big stupid kid that's break your neck in his hands. He gets drunk and into trouble. Seems to know the country real well. He's effective with a knife; not good or quick, just effective, like with his hands.

"Bert Grove, I guess, is the one you'd overlook, and die for it. I saw him once. Big, pale blond man, maybe thirty-five or forty, smart. This is his first big gang. Fairly fast with a gun—about as fast as you are, probably. He won't tighten up. Forget him in a fight and you'll regret it till your dying day —which could be right then."

He paused and looked at Jonathon. "Well?"

Jonathon's mouth had fallen open. "Heck fire! I didn't tell you that much!"

Phil shrugged. "You told me enough. When you depend on this." He patted his holster, "for a living, you remember things that might help you one day."

Jonathon grinned wearily. "And I was sweating!"

"It'd make it easier," Phil said, "if I knew who the people hiring me are."

Jonathon swallowed heavily. "I told you, Phil—"

"Sure," Phil snapped impatiently. "They're afraid maybe the word would get to Killian and they'd wake up dead. Forget it."

He had seen the first familiar land mark, a butte topped by a single, gnarled blackjack tree. It was the time to quit talking.

Phil left Jonathon at the fork of the creek and rode on alone. He rode through a blackjack woods, mottled with sunlight, and saw a snake hiss away, a woodpecker fly, and three crows circle and *caw* in alarm a hundred yards away. He wondered if there were still squirrels in the woods, and then he saw one dart across overhanging branches ahead. It was dry but cooler under the stubby trees, and he remembered other times here.

He rode out of the woods and down through a grassy pasture dotted with bushes. Beyond the next rise was the town.

His horse traversed the distance quickly. The wind felt good in his face as he topped the rise.

He had been away long enough that the town looked unfamiliar, although he could tell it had changed little. The crooked road bent into it, running between rows of frame buildings. Dusty trees swayed in the breeze. The sun shone brilliantly on the dusty streets.

The town was crowded. Horses and wagons clogged the main street, and he could see a big mob around the bank corner and the Golden Eagle saloon. The crowd milled constantly, and the way the people moved, too swiftly, too aimlessly to be casual, rang an alarm in his mind.

He knew at once that something was going on. Something unusual.

Nerves tightening, he clucked to his horse and started down the slope. He intersected the road just as it curved to slant into town. He passed one of the old water wells, and saw that it had been abandoned and covered with big rocks. Still someone—some kids, maybe, should have been there playing. It was deserted. A lizard shot under the rocks as he went past it.

He loosened his gun in its holster and slid the light glove off his right hand.

He rode past some new houses, stark, unpainted board homes with children's toys and the rubbish of living—a broken wagon wheel, a hammer, part of a plow—in the yards. He saw a curtain move quickly and knew someone had been watching him, and had jerked away when he looked in their direction.

Ahead, as the main part of town began, the street bent to the right. The dust of the people at the bank corner rose over the frame buildings, and he heard the rumble of voices. In a wagon parked beside the general store, he saw a woman and two babies. The woman was holding the babies close, looking tautly, gray-faced, toward the downtown.

Phil rode his horse to a hitching rack and dismounted. He wrapped the reins around the post and stepped up onto the board sidewalk under a tattered awning. The door of the barber shop beside him hung open, and the shop was empty. The benches on the sidewalk were bare, and store fronts stared out vacantly.

Phil walked toward the bend in the street, and turned it.

The crowd had converged on the Golden Eagle. The street was clogged with jostling men. Up on the porch of the saloon stood a man in a black coat, with ruffled shirt and a dark hat. Behind him, in the deep shade of the roof, stood two others. One, hatless, was blond and slender. The other, a tiny man with long arms and big hands, stood swaying gently as if he were ready to move violently.

Phil's memory registered. Killian. Grove. Brewster.

He turned the corner and walked nearer, holding to the sidewalk. Two rough-clothed men, farmers, stood at the edge of the hotel porch, watching from the rear of the crowd. Phil stopped just behind them. Someone in the front of the mob was talking to Killian. Phil couldn't see the man for those behind him.

One of the men beside Phil said, "Won't do no good."

"Might could," the other grunted. "Ever'body in town's signed it."

"Crap. Killian don't care fer a petition. He owns the water."

"He can't he'p but listen."

Phil edged by the men and to the back of the crowd. They were quiet, muttering and pushing against each other, craning necks trying to see and hear what was going on up at the porch.

"We can't take it no more!" a strident voice carried over the crowd. "We ain't payin' thet for water!"

Killian, his dark face seemingly emotionless under the brim of his hat, looked down at the man with a faint smile on his lips.

"I own the water," Killian said just loudly enough for all to hear. "I charge what I want to charge."

"It ain't fair!" the other man cried. "With the drouth an' all we can't pay it! You gotta come down."

Killian shook his head and looked out over the crowd. "I would like to cut the price of water, but it is impossible."

A rumble of anger went over the men at the sound of his precise, statesmanlike voice.

"I say let's string 'im up," a heavy-muscled man near Phil whispered.

"Gawd, if we could," another muttered.

"I didn't hear what he sed," another muttered. "What'd he say?"

The man at the foot of the steps looked up at

Killian angrily. "We ain't payin' it anymore, Killian," he said heatedly.

Killian stared down at him. "You have to. You have no choice. Unfortunately—"

"Damn that!" the man shouted. "We ain't payin'!"

Phil was shoved a few steps nearer the front as the crowd pressed nearer the porch. He looked around and saw anger, hesitation, almost unbelief, on the faces of the men near him.

So it was a demand for cheaper water, he thought. And it was getting nowhere. He wondered how high the water had to be for the people to get together this well.

But they hadn't gotten together well enough. They were sullen, beaten, not ready for violence.

"The water is an investment," Killian told the man at the steps. "It's expensive. If you are unable to meet your payment, I will be happy to make loans." He paused and looked over the crowd. "That goes for any of you. I know the summer has been bad. If you want loans, I can give them to you."

"Yeah," an angry man next to Phil said hoarsely. "Then we can't pay an' he gets our farms."

As he said it, he took a big step forward and shoved Phil through the crowd. Phil found himself in the front row, staring up into Killian's eyes.

Killian looked at him. "Now we all know how we stand," he said. "There is nothing more to say." He started to turn.

The little man, just a few steps from Phil, dropped the paper he held. His face drained of color.

"Killian!" he rapped.

Killian looked back, not fully turning.

"We ain't takin' it anymore," the little man choked. "We can't eat right 'cause we pay you fer water, an' it don't rain an' there's no crops.—We can't even leave 'cause we owe you."

The crowd murmured angry agreement.

Killian still had not turned all the way.

"We ain't gonna do it," the little man said doggedly. His face showed terror, but an even greater desperation. "If you're gonna keep it up—"

Phil saw the little man's hand tremble, and noticed for the first time that he wore an old Army gun stuck in the belt of his trousers. The wild look of his eyes told the rest. He was going to pull the gun.

Killian must have seen it too. His hand stole gentle across his chest, almost casually. Phil knew it was going for the Derringer.

"There's on'y one thing you understand—" the little man muttered.

Phil moved. If he didn't, the little man would be dead.

He sprang forward and swung his fist hard into his face. The little man's head snapped back and he groaned, dropping the gun that had just cleared his belt. Phil spun around to face the nearest man.

It was utterly silent.

He saw the nearest man's eyes go from him to a point beyond him on the porch.

He looked back.

Killian's gun was in his hand. Behind him, Brewster and Grove held leveled revolvers.

The little man got to his knees. His mouth trickled a stream of bright red. He looked at Phil dazedly.

"You don't want to die," Phil muttered.

The little man rubbed his face, and a sob tore

from his throat. "Don't make no diff'rence—can't live—"

Killian's voice cracked: "The meeting is over."

The men grumbled ominously.

Killian looked down at Phil. He didn't say anything, but Phil understood. He went up the steps onto the porch.

"Let's go," Killian said softly to his men.

They turned and went into the saloon. Phil followed them.

Luck, Phil thought. Maybe it was luck. He had saved the man's life, but maybe Killian would think it had been helping him. Now just introduce yourself. . . .

Killian smiled, his dark lips turning back from even white teeth.

"So happy to meet you, Mister Patterson," he said softly, extending his hand.

Chapter 5

PHIL hid his surprise at being recognized so swiftly. He took Killian's soft hand.

"You must have just arrived," Killian said, walking with him toward the bar. "You manage to get into the middle of things at once."

Phil glanced at Brewster's sickly, pock-marked face. He was watching closely, a strange hunger in his eyes.

"I thought he was going to get you in the back," Phil said.

Killian leaned against the ornate mahogany bar and tipped back his hat. "At any rate you saved us an ugly killing. We thank you."

Phil nodded.

Killian looked at his men. "Grove—Brewster—meet Phil Patterson."

Grove extended his hand and squeezed Phil's firmly. He grinned with a trace of lazy relaxation. "Coulda been some ruckus out theah. Yuh kep it down real nice for us."

Brewster extended a big cold hand and nodded without saying anything.

"I don't know what's going on," Phil said. "But there wasn't any use of gunplay."

"Another second," Brewster said harshly, "and I'd of kilt 'im."

Killian looked icily at his gunman. "And that would have made things worse, Brewster. Mister Patterson did it nicely."

A fat man in a white apron came from a back room and hurried along behind the bar. He pulled out a bottle and some glasses and put them in front of Phil, Killian and the others.

Killian poured drinks. He looked at Phil. "Are you here on business?"

"No," Phil lied. "Riding through."

Killian studied a heavy ring on his finger. "But this is your home."

Phil made a note that he had to be careful. Killian knew more than he had expected. "Yes. That's why I made it a point to ride this way."

As he said it, he looked at Brewster and Grove. Brewster had tossed off his drink, and stood hunched over, watching him intently. In the instant Phil looked at him, their glances meeting, he saw the thin edge of anger in the slit eyes, the tight-lipped mouth. Brewster was a killer, one who enjoyed it.

Phil knew Grove in the same moment. Grove politely kept his eyes on his glass as he turned it in clean, tapered fingers.

Phil didn't wonder who was faster. He knew that Brewster had to be. Brewster was the kind who didn't ever back down, so Grove must have done so or one of them would be dead.

Killian sipped his whiskey. "Do you plan to be here long?"

"I don't know," Phil parried.

Killian accepted it. "Redwater is a fine town."

"It looks like it's your town," Phil said.

Killian looked at him with the trace of a smile. "I'm a simple businessman."

Phil looked around the saloon. "Is this one of the simple businesses?"

"Yes. An investment."

Phil looked around the room, with its garishly framed pictures, heavy-painted walls, open timber ceiling. It had changed little under Killian's ownership, but it had always been the biggest and best place in town. It fitted, Killian owning it.

"Sometimes," Killian said slowly, wiping his dark hands with an immaculate linen handkerchief, "I find part-time work for men with spare time."

Phil put down his empty glass and shook his head as Killian started to refill it. It was a job offer, exactly what he wanted. But he couldn't look too eager.

"I may push right on through," he said slowly.

"If you decide to stay," Killian said.

Phil took his outstretched hand. "I'll let you know."

With a word to the others, he turned to the door and walked out.

He felt good. It was more than he could have hoped for. As he took his horse to a barn and put him up for the day, he wondered whether he should wait until morning to accept Killian's offer. The part he had to play was that of a gunman on the loose, ready for work of any kind, but cautious, just as suspicious as Killian had to be. Killian wasn't convinced at this stage that everything was smooth and as it should be; a man like that had to suspect everyone. Accepting the job too fast could throw more doubt.

The crowd had dispersed completely, and the

town appeared back to normal. Men sat on the shaded benches on the sidewalks, and others rode horses slowly along the main street. A farmer and his wife were loading a flat-bed wagon at the general store. Sweat trickled down Phil's back as he walked through the midday heat toward the hotel, and he knew when two men looked after him, whispering. No one spoke to him, and those who passed him on the sidewalk moved aside, to avoid his bulky saddle bags, without looking him in the eye.

It was about as he had expected. They wouldn't meet him with open hate, although they still felt it because he had let Michaels die. They wouldn't approach him openly because of his reputation.

The hotel, with its multiple balconies and white bric-a-brac trim, hadn't changed a bit. It looked across the angling street toward the town bank and, beyond that, the Golden Eagle. He turned into the double doors and walked across the lobby to the registration desk.

The clerk had a hairlip to go with scraggly black hair and a tweedy vest. His big eyes looked frightened as they took in Phil's low-slung gun and saddlebags.

"Yeah uhr?" he muttered.

"Need a room," Phil said.

The man shoved the registry book at him. "Bath key?"

Phil nodded and signed the book. He hesitated only a moment before going ahead and signing his right name. He paid for a day ahead and turned toward the steps.

The clerk's voice exclaimed: "Phil Pa'erson?"

Phil turned and looked at him stonily. "Something wrong?"

The clerk looked up wide-eyed from where he had just read the name in the register. "No sir!—No sir!"

Phil turned to climb the stairs.

After a bath and a change to his other clothes, Phil left the hotel and walked down the boardwalk in the cooler early evening air. He wasn't in a hurry, but he had decided to see Killian tonight. The tepid bath had taken the aches out of his legs, and a walk around town would keep them from stiffening up. But he hadn't walked halfway the length of the main street when he stopped.

Outside the blacksmith's shop stood a horse he recognized. It was a barrel-chested stallion with curious streaking of color along its fetlocks.

Phil felt a tingle of realization. It was one of Michaels' horses. It meant Cassie no, not at the blacksmith's—it meant Lester was there.

He turned quickly and headed back toward the Golden Eagle. He didn't know how Lester would take seeing him again. They had told him Lester was crippled from the gunfight that night; he limped, and couldn't work a full day's work. They had told him Lester still hated him. If he could avoid a meeting it might mean avoiding a fight.

Lester wasn't in the plan to bring him back against Killian. That much Jonathon had been definite about. "You have to take your chances with Lester," Jonathon had said.

He pushed into the Golden Eagle. The deep, narrow room had a few customers now. The gilded chandeliers had been lit, and glowed yellow over tables and chairs. The bar shone under the artificial light and a half-dozen men lounged against it. Two card games were going at back tables, and some of the women of the House were at others.

Phil saw this in his hesitation at the doorway. Without looking farther he walked to a table against the right wall and slid into the chair that gave him a view of the entire room. He nodded to the bar and then leaned his elbows lightly on the table, keeping his head down so he would appear tired, and paying no attention to what went on around him.

In reality he could see everything just under the brim of his hat. With his elbows lightly on the table he was in nearly ideal position to throw his gun—if he had to. Probably Lester wouldn't come in here—it was a gamble. It would have been more a gamble to walk the other block back to the hotel.

The bartender brought a bottle and glass. Phil paid him.

Two cowboys, their scrubbed faces shining eagerly, had invited two of the women to their table near Phil's. One was a blonde girl, perhaps twenty, in a blue satiny gown. The other, older and with red-dyed hair, laughed huskily as she draped herself over one boy's lap and messed up his plastered-down hair. Phil saw money change hands immediately, and the girls waved at the bartender. The boys were already weaving-drunk, and if the women could get them to pass out, it would mean profit without the formality of a trip upstairs.

But Phil's eyes only skipped over them. He looked to the back of the room again, where a door had opened for Killian, Brewster and a big lout that had to be Tub.

The three of them went to a table at the end of the bar and sat down. Killian said something and Brewster smiled. Tub laughed raucously, his big laugh filling the room raw and fresh, like the smell of manure. Phil knew they hadn't seen him, and lowered his head a trifle farther.

He turned back and watched Killian and the others. Killian was explaining something, ticking off points on his fingers and talking rapidly. Tub grinned foolishly and nodded, and Brewster's hand strayed to his gun and rested on the butt for a moment.

Phil catalogued the movement. Gummen, himself included, always touched their guns in the same motion used for the draw. It helped build good movement habits.

Brewster's elbow had crooked out slightly as he touched the gun, and his big hand went almost flat as he touched the butt. His thin body moved almost imperceptibly, but Phil caught it.

Putting the picture together he saw that Brewster moved on his draw, bringing his gun out away from his body as he stepped to the left, shooting from the side, presenting a side target and thumbing the hammer. He probably had a metal clip holster, the kind that opened up part-way in front so the gun would come out without being lifted all the way clear of the top. Probably the sideward movement went ahead of the hand movement by a split-second, because the way he crooked his elbow showed that his body was to be turned before he threw down.

It told Phil: *Draw on him when he makes a move to the side.*

The front door opened and he looked quickly to see.

Not Lester. Three cowboys, dust-coated from riding herd, stiff-legged, tired and grinning with anticipation of getting drunk. Red-necked and trailing dust behind them, they lined up at the bar.

The door swung open again, and Phil looked, expecting more cowboys.

The slim, sun-tanned man in black trousers and white shirt was Lester Michaels.

Temples thudding, Phil lowered his head a shade and watched.

Lester stood in the doorway, hands hanging limp at his sides. He wore a gun. His thin face looked strained and angry. His eyes scanned the room, coming toward Phil.

Phil lowered his head farther, blotting out his own vision. Lester had heard he was in town, and was looking for him.

Phil stared at his untouched glass and waited. The cowboys' voices came clearly over the muttered talk of the card players and the tinkling laughter of the women. Someone's glass clinked softly, and one of the women nearby said, "Well, dearie, don't pass out on us!"

Phil put his hand around his glass and raised it slowly. He put it to his lips and tilted his head back slightly, letting the hot liquid trickle down his throat. It gave him a chance to see Lester.

Lester had walked to the bar. He was leaning over it waiting hard-eyed to speak to one of the bartenders.

Phil looked toward the back. It was smokier now, but not confused enough for him to slip out unnoticed. He couldn't see a back door, unless the way Killian had come was the way outside. Killian and Brewster and Tub were still there, talking. If he went that way, he would have to stop by their table and that would give Lester all the opportunity he needed for recognition.

He thought of going to the bar and grabbing Lester tight by the arm so it caught his breath in surprise. Then maybe he could get him outside fast and have him under control. He thought of bolting for the door. Neither would work.

Again he glanced toward the back. It had to be that way.

He saw that one of the boys at the nearby table had passed out. His head rested on the table. The blonde in the blue dress was quietly slipping off his lap, smiling at the other boy, almost in a stupor too, as he held his girl tightly around the waist.

The blonde's eyes swept up and caught Phil's.

He beat down the impulse to look away. Maybe she was the way out.

He nodded to her and inclined his head, inviting her to join him.

Her breasts swelled as she took a breath, probably of resignation. It made no difference. She turned and walked toward him. She walked slowly, her legs outlining themselves against the satiny gown. She wasn't as pretty close as she looked at a distance, but she was pretty enough. She smiled down at Phil.

"Hello," she said.

"Sit down?" he asked huskily.

She took the chair beside him. Her knees bumped him under the table. Her half-bare breasts, heavily powdered and scented, made a tremble of sexual excitement go through him despite the situation. He met her gaze and saw crinkly cosmetics-lines around her eyes and mouth.

"Have you come far today?" she asked. She had a pleasantly husky voice.

"Doesn't matter," he said quickly. "Listen—"

"You need another drink," she smiled.

She started to turn toward the bar, but he caught her arm. She stared at him.

"Listen," he said urgently. "I don't want another drink, and I don't want what you think. Is there a back door out of this place from upstairs?"

She frowned. "Yes."

"I want to go up there," he said.

She smiled archly. "Of course."

"I don't want that," he gritted. "I'll pay you. Just get me up there without any commotion."

"What is this?" she demanded softly, her eyes darkening.

"How much?" he rapped.

"It depends," she began.

He slid three pieces of money across the table. "Enough?"

Her eyebrows raised as she looked. "Yes."

"All right," he said. "Now just make it look good. Make it look like we're going to your room."

She smiled and leaned over him. She took his hand and pressed it against her body and kissed him on the mouth. She took her face away slowly.

She said softly, "If you're in trouble—"

He stood, keeping his back toward the bar. "Let's get out of here."

She turned, slipping inside the ring of his arm. Awkwardly, rubbing together, they walked toward the stairs. It was the only way he could have walked sideways—with his back to the bar and Lester.

They went past the other woman at the table and she chuckled. Phil's nerves jangled as he wondered if Lester was watching. Past another table—almost to the steps—

A chair turned over behind him.

"Hurry," he bit out.

But it had been Lester turning the chair. His voice snapped:

"Wait!—Phil Patterson!"

The angry ring of his voice told Phil that there was no faking out of it. He let go of the woman's hand and turned slowly, ready, knowing that Killian was watching intently.

Chapter 6

LESTER stood three tables away. He swayed slightly, nostrils dilated, face ashen. His eyes had gone to pinpoints. His chest heaved under emotion. His thin wrists hung scarecrow-like from the once-rolled sleeves of his shirt. His right hand clenched and unclenched spasmodically. The only sound in the silence was that of the woman's shoes clicking on the stairs as she ran up them. The card players had stopped, and watched without daring to move. The men at the bar had turned, and watched, frozen. Killian, Brewster and Tub sat at their table. At the edge of his vision Phil could see Killian's slight smile and Brewster's keen-eyed attention. Brewster would be watching his draw.

"It *is you*," Lester breathed almost unbelievingly, as he went into a crouch.

"Hired gun for Killian here? Come back to finish the job you started letting my father die for you?"

"Shut up, Lester," Phil rapped.

Phil saw Killian's eyes narrow. He saw Brewster's hand slide two inches across the top of the table.

"I don't have any argument with you," Phil said desperately, fighting to keep it from coming to a head. "You'd better just be quiet."

Lester glanced back at the men on the far end of the bar. "You guys from South Texas? Take a look at Phil Patterson. He's tough. He's real good with a gun. He kills people."

No one said a word. The tension flooded out of Phil and a cold certainty replaced it.

He knew by a sense that he could not name that Lester would draw. He knew too that Brewster would draw at the same time, on Lester. He tensed, ready to leap at Lester.

Lester's hand became a claw. "Don't try it! Stay put! If you've got guts for anything beside old men and being Killian's stooge, come on!"

Phil saw both men at once. His back prickled. He could shoot Lester or watch Brewster do it. And Brewster would kill him.

"You scum," Lester breathed harshly. "You filthy Killian-man scum."

Brewster started to slide sideways on his chair. His hand went for his gun. Lester's hand jumped at the same instant.

Phil threw his gun and snapped a shot at Lester's shoulder. The gun boomed and the bullet splatted into Lester with a sound like meat being pounded with a hammer. He staggered and fell over backward against a table. The table slid away. He fell heavily, his gun clattering across the floor. Phil's shot echoed back across the room as Lester fell.

Phil looked at the fallen body over the smoke-curling barrel of his gun. Lester didn't move. Brewster's gun was in his hand, but he hadn't shot. Phil ignored the look in Brewster's eyes as he slipped his gun into the holster.

Sickened, he walked around the table to where Lester lay. He had to act absolutely indifferent. He fought to hide his emotions. If he had shot too low. . . .

Lester was breathing. The wound was low, but not too low. It welled bright blood, but there was no froth at Lester's lips. The bullet had missed the lung.

He looked around. No one had moved to help Lester. Their eyes showed nothing, but they were afraid to move.

All but Killian and Brewster and Tub. They didn't care.

Phil walked to their table.

"I could use a drink," he said harshly, fighting the inevitable reaction of a shooting.

Killian smiled. "Of course. Shall we go in the office?"

Phil turned to the card players. "He's not dead yet," he clipped angrily. "Maybe one of you can get a doctor if you're not too scared."

He turned and followed Killian into the back room.

Killian closed the door behind them, just the two of them. He motioned to a round table in the middle of the small room, where there was a bottle beside several glasses.

Without a word, Phil poured himself a stiff one and downed it.

Killian sat down opposite him. His eyes crinkled in a smile. "You're a good man with a gun."

Phil wiped his mouth with the back of his hand. "It's my living."

Killians poured himself a drink. "Michaels won't die."

"I shot too high."

"Purposely?"

"Of course not," Phil lied.

Killian's amber eyes gauged him. "You did not want him to die."

"All right," Phil snapped. "I didn't. He was a friend once. You don' t just kill friends."

"He would have killed you."

"Yes," Phil said, coming out in the open with it. "And your man would have killed him."

Killian's eyebrows raised slightly in surprise. "Yes. He would have."

Killian reached inside his coat and took out a thick wallet. With careful precision he counted a dozen paper notes, big ones. "I use Bank of Dallas money. It is very good money in Redwater. Everyone accepts it. I pay my men well. In advance. They take the money and take orders and do as I say."

He put the row of bills on the table. He met Phil's gaze.

Phil reached out and picked up the money. He folded it and slipped it into his shirt pocket.

Killian's teeth flashed. "You won't regret it."

He stood and went to the door. Opening it, he motioned. Brewster came to the doorway. Killian said something and Brewster nodded, glancing inside at Phil, and turned away.

"I want you to meet all the others," Killian said, returning to the table. "Then we will have a job for you."

Waiting for the others, Phil wondered how badly Lester had been hurt. He couldn't ask. He wondered too what job they had for him, and tried to imagine how he could find out about the hidden canyon. He was in now, but not established in their confidence.

The others came in one at a time, Grove first, then Brewster, then the hulking, good-natured Tub. The next man was Pop Schwartz, a dirty gray-haired man with a potbelly and tobacco juice stains out of the corners of his mouth. And last came Baxon, the insolent boy, wearing a bright red shirt with deep blue trousers and heavily-decorated boots.

Killian closed the door. "Meet Phil Patterson," he said simply. "He's going to be one of us."

Tub grinned stupidly. "I'm jus' as glad. Yur some bozo with thet gun, Phil."

"I heard they was some ruckus with Michaels," Baxon said in a high, nasal voice.

"Yeah!" Tub blurted. "Phil bored him good."

"He shot him high," Brewster said.

Phil looked around to see the little gunman leaning against the wall. His eyes looked cold and arrogant.

"That's right," Phil said. "I shot a little fast."

Brewster started to retort, but Baxon said unpleasantly, "Some night I'll finish what yuh started. I'll ventilate him good."

"That will hardly be necessary," Killian said coolly.

Baxon's eyes flashed. "I'm sick of thet bastard! I'll get 'im."

Pop Schwartz spat a stream of tobacco juice at a can, missed it, and raised his eyebrows disgustedly. He looked at Phil. "Seen the job yuh done on some cuss in Abilene a year'r so back," he said in a husky, whispering voice. "Real purty. Warn't an inch atween the holes."

"Funny," Brewster said caustically.

"What?" Schwartz rasped, turning.

Brewster grinned crookedly at Phil. "A man thet

can hit thet good shouldn't haf to shoot wild 'n hit a man in the shoulder."

Phil looked past Killian at the little gunman, and saw a dancing light in his eyes. It was excitement and greed—greed for action. The need to know. Phil's nerves started to draw up tight.

"That's not relevant at the moment," Killian said coolly.

"I'd say it's rel—relevant," Brewster said, the same vacant grin on his lips, his eyes not leaving Phil. "I'd say it's real important."

Killian looked at Brewster impatiently.

Brewster chuckled. "I'd say mebbe this ain't even Phil Patterson."

Killian's leg came off the edge of the table. Even Tub stiffened perceptably.

"Kinda hard to figger," Brewster said cunningly, leaning forward. "Is this the guy thet bored West Tidwell's eyes out in Dodge? Is this the guy faced down ole Poggin?—A guy can't even hit a cripple six steps away?"

A chair scraped behind Phil, and he knew Schwartz had moved out of the possible line of fire.

"Maybe I didn't want to kill Lester today," Phil said slowly. "Maybe it's better not to kill every man who gets drunk and wants to—"

"Crap," Brewster rapped. "You ain't Phil Patterson."

Phil stared at him. In the edges of his vision he could see Killian watching them tautly. The others had fallen back against the walls. Phil could see the look of rapt enjoyment on Baxon's warped young face.

But it was Brewster, Phil had to watch. Beads of perspiration glistened on his face. His mouth twitched nervously and his eyes caught the lamplight and gleamed yellow. He hadn't moved on the chair, but his body seemed to lean to the left. His throat worked convulsively. His yellowed teeth were gritted hard together. His whole body seemed stung to the breaking point, ready to explode. His hand had become a claw.

"You're wrong," Phil said softly. "Don't push it."

"You ain't Phil Patterson," Brewster clipped. "If you were, you'd of already throwed thet gun."

"Is that what you want?" Phil asked icily, hate rising like smoke in his brain.

"I'm gonna throw mine," Brewster whispered.

As he said it, his body started to fall to the left. His hand shot for his holster.

"Look out!" Grove barked.

Phil drew.

At the same instant Killian leaped with snakelike agility. Before Brewster's gun was clear, Killian's heavy body crashed into him. The chair broke with an explosion. Brewster hit the floor. Killian's hand swung around neatly and smashed into Brewster's face. Something popped. Brewster's face went crimson. He fell back, stunned. Killian scooped up his gun and whirled.

Phil stood frozen.

"Look," Killian rasped at Brewster. "*Look,* you filthy tramp!"

Brewster raised himself on one elbow and stared dazedly at Phil's big blue gun. Phil expelled his breath convulsively and holstered the weapon.

"He would have killed you," Killian snapped. "I should have let him."

Brewster wiped his bloody mouth. He looked at Grove.

Grove smiled slowly. "He's Phil Patterson,

Brewster. Y'all got any doubts?" He looked at the others.

Phil turned to face them, his blood still running hot. "Yes. Now's the time if any of the rest of you want to try. Killian won't be fast enough to save anybody else."

Baxon stood open-mouthed. "Geez. I never saw a gun move thet fast," he muttered in awe.

Phil looked at Schwartz. "How about you?"

Killian said quickly, "I don't think there will be more trouble."

"Did you hire me to kill your own men?" Phil rapped at him in genuine rage. "I've been in this town six hours and I've had it from both sides. Do you figure I'll take it?"

Killian's dark face flushed. "Your anger is justified. It won't happen again."

Brewster stood. He shot a flaming look at Phil.

"We can still go outside and find out," Phil gritted.

Killian turned on Brewster. "He's right. He'll kill you."

Brewster took his gun from Killian and looked at Phil uncertainly. He blinked and wiped fresh blood from his nose.

Phil stood ready.

Brewster dropped his gun into the holster and turned to drop onto a chair. His angry eyes stayed on the floor.

Grove rolled a cigarette. "Wal," he drawled with a grin, "thet's settled, an' we won't have no trouble. Okay, fellas?"

His soft southern tone injected soothing relaxation into the room. Phil met his eyes and saw the understanding, the steel, behind the smile. The smile and the eyes told him that they both knew

Brewster would have to try to finish it one day. But the look said too that they both knew Brewster wouldn't try it now.

Phil smiled grimly. "Can I borrow the makings, Grove?"

"Shore," Grove smiled, extending his tobacco and cigarette papers.

The crisis was past. Now Killian seated himself again at the table and motioned for Phil to sit down. His blood slowing and leaving him weak-kneed, Phil did so.

"If I had any doubts about your worth to us," Killian said slowly, "you just erased them completely."

Phil inclined his head, but said nothing.

"You have a temper," Killian said. "For the job I have in mind, you have to control it."

"I can," Phil said tightly.

Killian glanced at Brewster, then nodded. "Good. As you could tell today when you came to town, some of the townspeople have become difficult."

"It looked like you had them under control," Phil observed.

"So far," Killian agreed. "But if they become too aroused they might attempt to get a U. S. Marshal in here, and we can't afford that much trouble."

He stared at Phil. Phil asked, "How do I fit into it?"

Killian took a small cigar from his vest pocket and lit it carefully. He squinted through the smoke and looked around the room at his men. "Tub has uses, but you can tell he's crude. Baxon's youth sometimes irritates me. I thought for a time that

Grove might be the man I needed, but he isn't fast enough with his gun to frighten some people. Brewster is fast enough, but he can't be depended upon to kill the right person or at the right time. Schwartz is helpful, but not exactly awe-inspiring."

Phil watched each of the men as Killian spoke to them. Their eyes dropped before Killian's. Clearly this man was wholly in command. It made Phil reconsider his opinion. If Killian could keep them this much under control, he was very strong.

But Killian cut off further thought by continuing: "What I need is a man with Brewster's speed, Grove's intelligence and a good reputation. I think you might be that man."

Phil shook his head. "I have no reputation at all here. The old-timers hate my guts."

Killian smiled. "Of course. The old sheriff incident."

"They know my business," Phil said thickly.

"But if you renounced me openly," Killian said. "If you perhaps led some minor rebellion—made me lower the water rates."

Phil leaned forward. "What is it you're trying to set me up for?"

Killian flicked an ash from his cigar. "The town needs a sheriff."

Phil blinked. "Me?"

"Precisely."

Phil smiled, really smiling at the irony of being hired by both sides and playing the opposite role for each. But a pulse of interest made him reply, "You mean you want a man to run the town and make it look respectable so you can do as you please."

Killian smiled. "That's near it. You see, we can arrange for you to win a small victory over me—

one we have already planned—and then your election as sheriff becomes routine. It will not even require a vote. The people will assume you are keeping the town in fine shape, and we can expand to do as we see fit, making certain we don't do anything to embarrass you."

"What happens," Phil asked, "if there's trouble with your own men?" He glanced at Brewster.

Killian looked at the gunman too. "You kill them."

Brewster didn't blink or say a word.

Killian turned back to Phil. "Of course there are one or two men who couldn't be convinced by what we plan."

Phil saw what he meant. "Like Lester."

Killian nodded. "He is the number one man I had reference to."

Phil traced a pattern on the tabletop with his finger. "So?"

"So," Killian said, "Mister Michaels must meet with an accident."

"He may die from getting shot tonight," Phil said, tensing for what he knew was coming.

"No," Killian said. "But he can have another accident—any kind you wish."

"He's in bed someplace," Phil muttered.

Killian stubbed out his cigar. "Still he has to die."

Phil's stomach sank. "When? Who does it?"

Killian met his gaze. "Shall we say by tomorrow, at nightfall?—And of course there is only one man who can do the job properly."

Phil held his breath.

Killian stood. "It's your job. So if you please, see that Michaels is dead within twenty-four hours. Then we can get on to the rest of our plans."

Chapter 7

THE BLACKJACK woods lay utterly black under a moonless sky. Phil led his horse expertly, calling on faded memory. Bushes crackled dryly under his horse's hooves as he rounded a curve in the vague path and headed down into the declivity that was so familiar. A bird took wing with fright, flapping its wings loudly, and Phil clucked to his animal to reassure its jittery temper. The deep blue sky flamed with the light of a thousand western stars, and the cooler air hit Phil's sweaty body hard, chilling him.

Ahead, through the bush, he could see lights. Even the way the lights shone through the ragged foliage was familiar now, and he knew that it was his house, home, up ahead. He slowed his horse to a walk and proceeded carefully.

He saw as he neared the edge of the clearing that one light was in the house, while another was out at the barn. He could see movement through a crack in the barn door, and knew it must be Jonathon. He dismounted and walked carefully through the garden, smelling the dry earth and uprooted vegetables.

His feet scraped on the harsh earth outside the barn door, and it sprang open swiftly. Jonathon stood there with the lantern in his hand, staring wide-eyed into the darkness.

"It's me," Phil said huskily.

Jonathon lowered the lantern. "Come inside," he said.

Phil stepped into the straw-floored barn and swung the rickety door shut behind him.

Jonathon brushed dust from his clothes and studied Phil's face. "What's up? Are you in trouble?"

Phil told him in a few words.

"Gawd," Jonathon breathed, sinking to a bale of hay. "You're in the gang, aw right, but you can't kill Lester!"

"I know it," Phil rapped. "I need help."

"You think we should try to explain to him what's going on?"

"I don't know what else to do," Phil said. "Do you have any other ideas?"

Jonathon rubbed his face. "I dunno if he'll believe us."

"He'll have to. We have to make him."

Jonathon swallowed heavily. "What're we gonna do to convince Lester?"

Phil looked around at the familiar bare wood walls of the barn. "I don't know. Where is he, do you know?"

"Yeah. Cassie said they brang him home. You caught him high up in the arm. He ain't hurt bad."

The mention of her name sent a tingle through him. "Was Cassie here?"

"Yeah," Jonathon said, looking toward the house. "She's up there now."

"Now?" Phil echoed.

"Yeah. She come over about a half-hour ago."

Phil stared at his grimy hands.

"What's the matter?" Jonathon asked. "You scared she'll see you here?"

"No," Phil muttered. "No. I'm not—I mean—how is she?"

Jonathon grinned foolishly. "She's purty excited 'bout what happened. Kinda mad. Says Lester ain't got no call to come back at you that way."

Phil licked dry lips. He wondered what she looked like now, after so many years, a husband, being a widow. His insides went weak and he felt sick and wanting to see her. He remembered time here—right in this barn—when they stood close together, hot and sweaty. Puppy love, maybe, but all of it good and true and hurting-clean, wanting all of it, and she crying finally, and running from him, and then coming back, her great wild eyes soft and tender and brimming.

His hands balled into fists. His knuckles cracked.

"Maybe," Jonathon said slowly, "we could explain it to her."

"No," Phil snapped.

"Heck," Jonathon said. "That's the best way, maybe. She could tell ole Lester."

"No," Phil repeated. "She doesn't get in this in any way."

"Heck, Phil—"

"That's it," Phil rapped.

Jonathon scuffed his boot into the dirt. "Okay. I jus' thought—"

"We leave her out of it."

"Okay, Phil, okay! What do we do?—I mean, do you just ride over and tell Lester yourself? What if he pulls a gun on you, or somethin'?"

"He'll be in bed," Phil said. "I'll take care of it. You just make sure Cassie—" His voice choked on the name—"Cassie isn't going to be there. Get her to meet you to go to town or something."

"It'll be hard," Jonathon said reluctantly.

"Do it," Phil said shortly.

"Yeah," Jonathon said. "Sure."

"We have to—" Phil began.

But he got no further.

A sweet clear voice called from right behind him: "Jonathon? Where are you?"

Cassie.

He turned, his eyes racing around for a place to hide. But it was too late.

The barn door swung open and he saw the flash of calico dress, then the outlines of her body. Then she stepped into the full light. Her auburn hair glowed. Her creamy skin shone in the light. She was about to say something, and then her eyes went from Jonathon to him. Her lips remained parted. She said nothing. Her breath came in a tiny spasm of surprise. An ivory hand went to her throat.

Phil smiled in bitter resignation. "Hello, Cassie."

"Phil?" she faltered.

She stood transfixed, one smooth hand at her throat. Her bare arms were round and soft. She was as he had remembered her, but infinitely more lovely. The lithe lines of her body made his throat hurt with her beauty. He saw the tiny scar at the corner of her mouth where she had cut herself on his knife when they were twelve. The scar only enhanced the smoothness of her skin, the fragile delicacy of her face. Her hair just touched her shoulders, and had been combed to a burnished luster. Her simple dress swelled over womanly breasts, tucked in at a tiny waist, smoothed snugly over rounded hips. Older, more a woman, but the same Cassie. The one he had never forgotten, the one who had nevertheless become hazy in his mind.

She recovered partially and stepped on into the barn, closing the door behind her. "I knew you were in Redwater," she faltered. "Lester—"

Phil nodded. "I came back."

That sounded dumb, he thought numbly. He didn't know what to say.

Cassie smiled uncertainly. "Well, you certainly look—look like you always did."

He met her eyes. "How's Lester?"

She swallowed. "He's all right—he'll be fine.—It was so stupid of him."

"Maybe not," Phil said. "I can understand the way he feels."

"That's—far behind us," she said softly.

"Maybe so," he said. "I often wondered—"

She cut in quickly, "We can make Lester understand."

Phil smiled bitterly. "If I hadn't understood exactly what he does, I would have never left Redwater."

"That's all in the past," she protested.

"Yes. I guess a lot's happened. I hear you were married."

A deep blush colored her face. "Yes. I'm—there was an accident—"

"I know," Phil nodded. "I'm sorry."

"You learn to accept," she said simply.

He looked up at her.

She met his look for a second. Then she turned to Jonathon as the restrained excitement of the moment threatened again to suffuse her face.

"Jonathon," she said, striving to be matter-of-fact, "your mother wants you to bring the eggs from the bin."

Jonathon nodded. "I was anyway."

She looked back at Phil. She didn't seem to know what to say. There was an awkward silence.

Jonathon coughed nervously. "Hey, how about goin' in the house? You ain't seen maw yet, Phil."

"In a minute," Phil said, fighting for self-control.

Jonathon grinned nervously. "You want I should go on?"

"I guess so," Phil said huskily. "Maybe tell her I'm on my way out. Maybe she needs to get ready or something."

Jonathon nodded and went out of the barn.

Cassie looked down at Phil with her heart in her eyes. "She doesn't need time to get ready, Phil. She's been cleaning house all day long for you."

"I need a minute myself," Phil said. He looked up at her and wished to hell she wasn't so pretty. "It's been a long time since I've been home."

She forced a smile. "I thought men didn't worry about home, and things like that."

"Maybe others don't. Some things never stop bothering you. Me, maybe I should say."

"Why didn't you ever come back?" she asked softly.

"You ought to know," he said.

"My father?"

"Of course."

"But that's forgotten. We know what you had promised."

"I let him die."

"It worked out the way it did because it had to," she said earnestly.

He tilted his head to meet her gaze. "Maybe so, Cassie. What I've become since then makes it impossible anyway."

"A gunman," she said tonelessly.

He didn't answer.

"You've—killed many?"

"Seven," he bit out ruthlessly. "Seven men. That doesn't count any I'm not sure of."

She shuddered. "Phil."

"So you see why I couldn't come back," he said, forcing himself to grit it between his teeth. "Some men have blood on their hands. I've got it all over me. Some people have killed a lot more. Seven is plenty. I could have killed a dozen more if I wanted to—every stinking little town has a hero who wants to try a big-time gunman."

"But you've come back now," she protested.

"Yes," he agreed, dry-throated. "I have a job."

"With Killian."

"With Killian."

"It's wrong."

He stood to meet her at an even level. "I imagined you and Killian were—good friends."

She dropped her eyes. "Since—since my husband's death, Mister Killian has been—very kind."

"What do you think of him?" He didn't want to ask, but it was like the admission of killing. Goaded, he had to say it. "Do you like him?"

Her face was pale. "I—don't know. He's always been good to me, but—he just doesn't seem really as nice as he acts."

"You know he's selling water and running the Golden Eagle."

"Yes," she said, surprising him with her candor. "And I know he sleeps with one of the women he keeps at the Golden Eagle, too."

He blinked. It was another sign, a surprise show of her maturity, the fact that she was not the woman he had left. It emphasized the gap between them. He didn't know what to say.

"I hope you're not going to keep working for him," she said softly.

He swallowed. "I don't know if I will or not."

She fidgeted with her hands, twining them nervously. Finally she said hesitantly, "We're—glad you're back."

A ball of sour dough rose up in the back of his throat. He thought for an instant he was going to bawl like a kid. He sniffed and wiped his nose. He wanted to take her in his arms. The hunger for her was so strong he didn't know if he could resist it.

She turned slightly, breaking the spell.

"We'd better go see your mother," she said huskily, and started to the door.

"Cassie?" he choked.

She turned, a vision in the calico, with her bare arms round and firm. Her lips parted. "Yes Phil?"

He stared at her.

She waited.

He choked it back. "Nothing. Maybe we'd better go to the house—like you said."

Chapter 8

IT WAS between nine and ten in the morning when Phil left the hotel in town and started circuitously toward the Michaels ranch. Already the sun glowered hot in a bronze sky, and dust rose on the trail to stick to his sweaty face. His goal had to be convincing Lester, and this was a good time to see him alone. With Jonathon keeping Cassie busy in town, and the hands out on their morning rounds, Lester very well could be alone in the house.

It was even more important for Lester to be alone, or poorly protected, if attempts at convincing him failed. If Lester wouldn't believe Phil's real reasons for being here, and quit fighting him, there was only one other thing to do: get him out of the way.

On the chance that this became necessary, Phil had checked to make sure his and Jonathon's old hunting shack was still standing in the gulch. It would be perilous, trying to get Lester there, but it was the only other thing to do if he wouldn't believe the truth.

Phil didn't attempt to keep to the woods or stay out of sight. After he left town and cut back onto the trail toward the Michaels house, he rode openly. There would be no chance to get all the way to the house unnoticed anyway; not if luck was bad. The house had been built near the face of a granite cliff, facing a natural glade. Unless you scaled the cliff or took the long way through the canyon and rode the cliff-wall trail, you couldn't get within two hundred yards of the house without riding across open grass.

So Phil rode easily, and in the open, as if he had nowhere in particular to go. He sat his saddle relaxed, as if his insides weren't strung tight with anticipation.

He had gotten into Killian's gang more easily than he had expected, but they didn't fully trust him yet. The idea of being Killian's sheriff was perfect for Phil's own goal. Killian would have to let him know what the gang was doing so he wouldn't blunder into them at the wrong time and lose face as sheriff, when he didn't arrest them. But Lester was the problem. Lester could raise so much hell that everything would be ruined.

Killing Lester, of course, wasn't really necessary from Killian's standpoint. Phil knew that. It was a test. Killian knew they had been friends. If Phil killed him as ordered, it would signal to Killian that old friends meant nothing to a professional gunman, a killer who was at his command.

So Lester had to be convinced, and talked into disappearing for a while, or else he had to be made to disappear by force. After he was out of the way, Phil could say he had killed him. Then Killian's trust would be gained, Phil could become the phony sheriff, and the secret of the canyon—and perhaps other secrets—would be near discovery.

Turning his horse down the ravine that led nearer the ranch house, Phil thought of the night before, and of the reunion with Cassie and his mother. It had been a bittersweet meeting. His mother had aged, shockingly so. Her hair was all gray now, and she had lost weight until her face was pinched like the skin of a man caught in the cold for a long time. And the house hadn't changed except to grow older and seemingly smaller, the same furniture, the same walls looking more faded, more poor. He couldn't know how much of the change was real, and how much was simply evident to him for the first time, after being away so long.

But his mother's joy at seeing him had been unmistakable. A hesitation in her speech, an undefinable sadness in her eyes, showed how keenly she felt his occupation and past. But she had laughed with him, and gently kissed his cheek, and repeatedly looked from him to Jonathon and sighed and said, "Both my boys home."

Now his horse climbed slowly up the incline out of the gulch, and cantered through the woods nearer the house. In another moment—yes. Phil could see it through the thinning brush.

It hadn't changed much. The low, long frame house nestled back against the face of the cliff. Lilacs grew thick and green around the wide, freshly-painted front porch, and a new stone wall had been built around the well. But the six wide windows, built to catch the south breeze, looked the same, as did the wall of blackjacks separating the house from the barns and outbuildings. The trees had grown; he couldn't even see the other buildings although he knew they were there. He remembered how the elder Michaels had spoken of the day when those trees would grow big enough to cut off the working area of the ranch from the house.

Phil had helped transplant the trees. He had never, he thought wryly, imagined that he would be taking advantage of the setup, hoping he could get to the house without being seen.

But if he was to get there unseen, it would take luck.

He looked toward the trees separating the barns and corrals from the house, and he thought he could hear men's voices. A trace of woodsmoke touched his nostrils, clean and warm. The sun baked down on the grass and he noticed how burnt and brown it was. Even around the well the grass was parched and dead.

He rode to the steps of the porch and dismounted in the shade. He tossed the reins over the hitching rail. The wind brushed the lilacs, bringing out of them a wet green smell, proof that they had been watered. The new paint on the porch smelled oily and clean, rich. Front curtains in the house moved in the breeze, but there was no other movement.

His steps sounded loud on the porch. He crossed to the door, going around the old mahogany-colored glider with red and blue cushions on it. He peered in through the screen. It was too dark. He couldn't see a thing.

He pulled the screen door open and stepped into the house.

It was the living room. Memory flooded back, but Phil didn't have time to stare. If he was alone now, it wouldn't be for long.

He walked lightly across the living room and into the corridor that led to the bedrooms. The first room's door stood open, and the heavily-shaded room was empty. The bed had been made neatly. Cosmetic items and a faint odor of flowers told him it was Cassie's room.

He stepped to the next door. It was partly closed. He touched it gently with his hand and it swung open.

Lester lay in a big double bed covered with a red and white quilt. Beads of sweat glistened on his face and chest, but he was sleeping. The room was still, stuffy and dark as night.

Phil swallowed and stepped into the room.

"Lester," he said softly.

Lester's forehead wrinkled in a frown, as if he were dreaming. One of his hands went to his face and brushed at it. The quilt fell farther back and Phil saw the clean bandages on his upper arm.

"Lester," Phil said a trifle louder.

Lester's eyes opened. He stared at the ceiling. Then he turned to look toward the door, toward Phil. For a moment he stared, blank-eyed. Then recognition lit his face.

"You here?" he choked.

"Listen," Phil said, taking a step toward the bed. "Be quiet. Maybe you won't believe—"

A convulsive movement under the quilt gave him a split-second's warning. Lester's hand shot under the pillow and swung back to the front. A gun. The gun blasted the silence in the room and an orange flame shot out at Phil's face. Something like a sledge-hammer smashed into his chest. He was hurled back against the wall. He reeled, the pain and the hot smell of powder reaching his brain simultaneously.

He didn't lose consciousness. He fell across a chair and pain seared into his body as he fell to the floor. He thought racingly, *They'll hear the shot, you have to take him now and fast.*

As he hit the floor he turned over and came up on his knees beside the bed. Lester swung the big gun toward him, toward his face at six inches away, but the hesitation was long enough for Phil to grab the gun by the hot barrel and slam it down onto the mattress. It went off, muffled by the covers.

Phil sprang to his feet. Lester tried to roll. Phil brought his elbow down in an arc, throwing his whole weight behind it. He connected perfectly to Lester's jaw and Lester's head snapped over backward under the impact.

But he didn't go out. His feet shot up into Phil's stomach and only a desperate wrench to the side avoided them. Phil jerked out his gun and sliced it down across Lester's temple. The barrel hit hard, but a glancing blow. Lester's head ripped under the impact and blood spurted. He fell back, as if dead.

Phil drew a shuddering breath and stood limp-armed, looking down at Lester. Then he looked at his wound. It had started sending hot pains through his torso. He couldn't tell much because the bullet had gone in below his shoulder, taking bits of his shirt with it. The wound was jagged and bleeding freely, disgorging chunks of material out of his shirt.

His knees went weak and he sank to the bed. The house was utterly silent, but it wouldn't be silent for more than another minute.

He reached up and ripped a pillowcase off one of the pillows. Quickly he folded it into a bulky pad. He tore two buttons off his shirt as he struck the pad in on top of the bullet hole. Crimson had already puddled on the bed sheets.

It didn't feel like anything was broken. It hadn't begun to hurt as bad as it would later, when the shock started to subside. He could move, and right now he had to move fast.

Awkwardly he hoisted Lester up onto his good shoulder. Swinging the body sideways he got it through the door and down the hall. He looked hurriedly out the front door. He saw no one. He staggered outside and down the steps to swing Lester onto the back of his horse. He swung up to the saddle and dug spurs. The animal lunged powerfully and hit his stride down the narrow path beside the house, cutting around a hedge and into the brush beside the cliff.

Behind him he heard shouts. He didn't dare look back. The rushing confusion of the ride demanded every ounce of his attention. Going the back way was longer. He had to hit down into the riverbed and cross somewhere, probably Eagle Bend, six miles down. Then across to the shack.

His horse was running wild, picking his own route. A fallen tree loomed in the path, and the shock of ride stopped for a long instant as they hurdled it, then hit again hard, running. Phil reached down to grab Lester's body more securely.

Something smashed across his chest. Blue pain blinded him. He hurtled backward off the saddle, hanging in the air. He fell. He hit falling on his side, dust scooped into his mouth and the earth tore flesh from his chest as he skidded. His breath was gone and he looked up through haze to see the horse plunge wildly away, down the trail.

For an instant he didn't move. His chest was crushed. He couldn't draw air. He was collapsed inside. The hot fire of strangulation closed in and he fought, but he couldn't suck in air. The pain of steel bands on his chest, holding him, struck deep into his vitals. He clawed at the dirt and looked up in agony.

He saw Lester's body lying less than ten feet away.

A gasp of air sucked into his lungs.

Slowly, agonizingly, he fought to expand his chest. He groaned as air pushed grudgingly inside him. The world was trimmed in deep red and he couldn't feel anything but the pain in his chest.

Then his lungs ballooned. His heart pounded like a trip-hammer. A hot flush poured through him. Sweat burst from his pores.

A faint sound toward the house jerked his nerves to attention.

They would be coming.

He rolled to his hands and knees. Slowly, with effort, he stood.

The world rocked beneath his feet, but he gritted his teeth and held on. He sucked in air until it hurt so strongly he couldn't hold it. He expelled air and opened his eyes.

Things had come into focus. He looked up and saw a thick, crooked branch that had swept him out of the saddle. The impact had broken leaves and small branches off it, but it still hung there solid. He was lucky it hadn't killed him.

Lester groaned and moved.

Phil knelt beside him and rolled him over. He hadn't caught the impact. The blood had started to coagulate on the side of his head, and his eyelids fluttered. His face was very white.

"Lester," Phil hissed.

Lester's mouth opened and closed and one arm moved. He groaned again.

"Lester," Phil rapped, shaking him.

The man's eyes opened blankly.

Phil pulled his gun and leveled it on him. "Get up."

Lester stared at him. Recognition crept in behind his eyes like shadows behind the curtains of a house at night. He didn't move. He licked his lips.

"Get up," Phil said grimly. "Fast!" He thumbed back the hammer of his gun.

Lester didn't say anything. He scrambled to his feet and stood there, swaying. His hands went to his head and he squeezed his skull at the temples as if trying to keep it from flying apart.

Phil stepped in close to him. "Listen. We're climbing the cliff. You go first. Try anything and I'll kill you. Get going."

Lester stared hot-eyed at him, then at the gun. He looked back down the trail.

Phil motioned with the gun. "Now, damn it!"

Lester turned to the face of the cliff. He reached up and grabbed a bush with his good arm and started pulling himself up.

Phil started up right behind him, into the scrubby vegetation. The cliff here was steep, but not too steep for climbing. Through the pain in his chest and shoulder he thought vaguely that he and Lester had done this before, climbing all of it, as kids.

It wouldn't be a tough climb in good shape. Lester's boots scuffed loose red dirt back onto him as they panted higher, inching their way, still making good time. But beyond this dirt slide was the rocky part. That wouldn't be easy with two good arms between them.

Lester looked back down at him, cold hate in his eyes. "What do you think you'll gain doing this?"

"Keep going," Phil grunted, pulling himself nearer.

Lester changed direction slightly, angling along a rutted ditch made by spring rains. "You get up here, what do you have? There's no place to go."

"We'll go across the bridge," Phil said hoarsely.

"You're crazy!"

"Maybe I am. That's where we're going."

Over the scuffing and weed-breaking he heard something else.

"Hold it!" he rapped.

Lester stopped, falling onto one hip on the incline.

Phil turned his head partway, keeping Lester within his vision.

Fifty yards below, coming down the trail, were five men on horseback. They plunged ahead recklessly, spurring their horses.

Phil waggled the gun at Lester in mute warning.

The men bolted up to the low-hanging branch. The first two ducked under it. The third looked down and saw the blood in the dust. He shouted. They reined up, horses pawing air and dancing nervously in tight circles.

Through the melee Phil recognized two of the men. One, black-haired, big and strong-looking, his arms sticking out of the tattered sleeves of a cut-away flannel shirt, was Steve Jennings, Michaels' old foreman. Another, a wiry man with a black hat, was Jack Schaefer, one of the top hands. It was Schaefer who had spotted the blood. He sprang from his mount in an effortless swing and squatted beside the spots.

He touched them with his hand. He looked up to Jennings.

"Fresh," he said clearly.

Jennings looked around, turning his horse. "I don't see any sign."

"He stopped," Schaefer grunted.

"Must've gone on."

"Maybe he took out through the brush."

"Uh-uh. Ain't broke up."

"Er up the cliff."

All of them craned their necks.

Phil froze, his thumb drawing the hammer back on the gun.

The men squinted out of the bright sunlight of the trail. The cliff-side lay in deep shadow.

Bushes partly obscured Phil's position, and he knew they couldn't see unless Lester moved or cried out. His thumb drew the hammer back a fraction more. He looked at Lester out of the corner of his eye, meeting his gaze.

The knowledge communicated between them: *Tell them and I kill you.*

The men stared up into the shade, squinting hard. A bird wheeled over them in a lazy arc and a beetle crawled past Phil's shoulder in the dirt. The creak of saddle leather as the horses moved was the only sound.

Jennings looked down and rubbed his neck. "Hell. What'd they go up there for? Les couldn't climb it anyway."

Schaefer nodded. "Nowhere to go, I guess."

"They're up ahead," Jennings said. "If we don't catch up by the river, we can split up. Two go to Eagle Bend, one back here, two up the far side of this thing. If they're up on that cliff, they ain't nowhere they can go."

"How about over the bridge?" one of the others asked.

Jennings spat. "Nobody ever made it acrost yet, buster."

They touched spurs and slammed down the trail.

Phil waited until the sound of hoof-beats had

faded. The dust sank slowly in the air, making rainbows in the sunlight. The wind sighed. He looked at Lester.

"Up," he said.

"You're crazy," Lester repeated. "We can't make it across there."

"Up," Phil repeated harshly. The pain was making him mad.

Lester turned and started up again.

It took ten minutes to get to the top. Jagged rock cut deep into their legs and arms, and Phil's shoulder was driving him crazy with shooting pains that went clear into his back. The front of his shirt was sopping red. He kept his eyes glued on Lester, grabbing the same holds he had used on rock and branches, letting everything but Lester blur out as they climbed back into sunlight. They angled up the face of the cliff and then they were at the top.

Climbing to their feet, they stumbled forward in the shrill high wind. Bushes leaned in the cool and clean breeze. There weren't any trees. They were high up.

Then they were on the other side: at the bridge.

It wasn't big. The natural rock formation arched up, linking this chunk of earth with the face of another cliff thirty yards away. It was wind-rounded and smooth, no thicker than a big tree, sand-colored, with gleaming bits of granite. A natural bridge, one so narrow and high they had never thought of crossing it even as kids, when they would do almost anything.

Below, farther below than the trail they had climbed from, lay the river gorge.

Jagged rock walls seemed to fall away backward to the thin-looking streak in the rock that was a river. This side, cut deep by that plummeting water, was over three thousand feet straight down.

Lester turned from the chasm. The wind caught his torn shirt and flapped it like a scarecrow garment. His face had gone white. He licked dry lips.

"We can't make it, Phil," he muttered. "I won't try it."

Phil motioned with the gun. "You'll try it."

Lester looked back at the slender column of rock vaulting out over the gorge. He shuddered. "No."

Phil didn't think of turning back. The only way to the shack now was over that wobbly-looking rock formation—over the three thousand foot drop—and along the far ridge. From the far side it wasn't thirty minutes' walk.

"Where are we going?" Lester asked huskily. "What the hell are you doing?"

Phil wiped his face with his hand. He hurt all over. "You won't believe it anyway, Lester. I'll tell you, though. Killian hired me to kill you."

Lester laughed hysterically. "And you haf to shove me off that bridge?"

"No. I don't want to kill you. He has to think I did. I'm taking you to our old fishing and hunting shack. Jonathon's going to keep you there."

Lester again shuddered. "I'm not going over—that."

"We're going over," Phil snapped. "We're doing it my way."

Lester suddenly slumped before his gaze. "All right," he said chokingly.

They walked to the edge of the cliff, where the natural bridge jutted out from solid rock formation. It was perhaps four feet thick at the base, and narrowed to less than three feet as it spanned the gap.

Lester walked up to it, then paused. He looked at Phil.

"Go ahead," Phil said. "And if you try anything—"

Lester nodded. "We both go."

"Go on," Phil prodded woodenly.

Lester slipped his leg over the smooth, round rock. He sat down on it. He looked at Phil.

Phil leveled the gun on him. Everything blurred, then snapped back into sharp focus.

Lester reached out and grabbed his good arm tight around the rock and shinnied forward two feet. He stopped and pulled his legs up to his body and moved forward again.

Phil's throat got a sick feeling in it as he slipped his leg over the cold rock as Lester had done, and leaned forward on the smooth, weather-beaten surface. He felt the rock tremble under the wind. He slipped his gun into its holster and pulled himself forward.

He was out over the gorge. The blurry rock an inch from his face again trembled. He held, sickeningly afraid, his stomach floating free. His hands groped forward and he pulled, his shirt sliding along the rock. He looked up ahead and saw Lester inching along. Lester was a fourth of the way across, higher than he now, nearing the top of the curving rise.

Phil's bloody hands slipped on the rock for a split-second and he froze, hugging the rock with his elbows and knees. His head reeled and he thought he would fall, but then he gnashed his teeth together and hung on and forced himself to get control.

He looked back. He had come ten feet.

He looked down. The earth fell out from under

him. Down—far down—was the roaring ribbon of the river. He saw a bird swoop through the sky below him, below the hanging heels of his boots. The rock walls of the canyon sloped away into blurring infinity and he sucked in a breath as his insides lurched to come out.

He looked back at his one hand, crimson-splotched on the knobby-smooth stone in front of his face.

This was reality, he told himself dazedly. This was something to hang onto—he had to hang on to it—and move.

He looked up the sloping cylinder and saw Lester at the top, staring back at him. The wind had his shirt tail whipping against the glass-blue sky.

He had been afraid before, but never like this. Other times it had been men he was afraid of or worried about. That had been fair and real, and if he had died, he knew what that death would be like.

He didn't know what it would be like to hurtle down sickeningly through space. He wondered if you felt the fall, or whether you just hung there and everything else moved.

One slip—he swallowed again—one slight wrong movement—and he wouldn't be able to hold. He would go on over and fall free, going upside down—

He stared hard at the rock. He moved again, desperately aware of his boots digging in and slipping back against the bridge. He held so tight his back ached worse than his shoulder. There wasn't any going back. He was hanging in space, and could only go forward.

His hands and legs moved woodenly, of their own volition. He fought himself to keep from hurrying. Slowly—slowly—

The rock trembled again. He lay flat, hugging the stone to himself.

He was over the peak. It was downhill.

He saw Lester ahead of him, nearer than before, inching along. He was hardly moving. He was clutched to the rock, his mouth was open and he was crying. He was staring back at Phil.

"Keep going!" Phil shouted hoarsely. "You're almost there!"

He didn't look to see if Lester complied. He looked beyond him to see the far end of the bridge —and the rocky platform off the end of it.

He drew his legs up again, carefully, and reached his clawing hands forward. He pushed gently and slid another foot nearer to safety.

The wind shrilled higher and he cursed bitterly. It was so near now—just a dozen movements ahead—and the rock trembled.

He took another slide forward. Eleven to go. He saw Lester moving too, nearer, going faster, almost recklessly, sobbing.

"Get on off!" he roared at the top of his voice. "You're almost there!"

His cheek lay against the cool stone. He heaved a deep breath.

Nine to go—no slips—eight—

He saw Lester tumble off the end of the bridge and roll onto the rock platform. He had made it.

This wasn't the place to get careless. The chasm below lay just as deep as it had at the middle. The bridge had thickened slightly, but that only made it harder to squeeze with his wide-pulled knees. His trousers had already been torn open by the chafing crawl forward, and his skin was raw. Keep going—just a couple more feet—one more big lunge, no, two, slow, careful, small advances—

The gorge disappeared. Dusty rock lay under his feet.

He rolled off the cylinder and hit beside Lester. He lay exhausted, his chest heaving. His hands stung like fire. He looked back the way they had come, at the spindly bridge of stone.

Impossible, but they had crossed it.

He swallowed, and the sick feeling was gone. He pulled himself to watery legs and stood.

"Get up," he said in a choking whisper. "We've still got a walk ahead of us."

Chapter 9

THE MAIN STREET of Redwater blurred out of focus as Phil rode toward the Golden Eagle. He held himself erect in the saddle, trying to look unconcerned. People were staring at him and he knew they could see the crimson stains on his chest and back, but he tried to sit as if he weren't hurt. Jonathon's horse had a soft walking gait, or he might not have made it.

As it was, he reeled out of the saddle into Schwartz and Grove's arms at the saloon. They dragged him inside through the back way, and he hardly knew what they were doing.

They half-carried him into the small back office. Phil heard a chair go over, then saw Killian looking down at him. They had laid him on the floor.

"What happened?" Killian demanded.

Phil swallowed. "He had a gun in bed with him."

Grove expertly ripped his shirt back and probed gently at the wound, sending ribbons of fire through his body.

"Clean's a whistle," he muttered. "Nothin' broke."

"Drink," Phil muttered.

Schwartz handed him a glass of whiskey, and held his head up to help him drink it. It went down hot and clean, spreading through him with new strength.

"You failed, then?" Killian asked grimly.

Phil shook his head. "I shot him. I hauled his body to Salt Cliff and dumped it."

"With that hole in yuh?" Grove asked incredulously.

Phil looked at him. "I thought it would be better —if they didn't know what had happened."

Killian interrupted: "You weren't seen?"

"No," Phil muttered.

Killian's eyes gleamed. "You did it the right way." He sounded proud and satisfied. He looked at Grove.

Phil said huskily, "I need some cutting done. The slug's still in there."

"Get Baxon," Killian's voice rapped.

"I'll get the Doc," Schwartz said.

"No. We can't trust him. Baxon can cut it out."

The pain lessened and Phil opened his eyes. Killian and Grove were looking down at him.

"That was good thinking," Killian said admiringly, "taking the body."

"Yeah," Grove snorted. "Guess we din't need anyone watchin' him, eh boss?"

Phil's jagged nerves tingled. "Watching me?"

"We sent Baxon out to follow you," Killian said. "In case you needed help, of course."

"He heard the shot from the woods," Grove said lazily. "He lit out, 'n waited for yuh down the trail. You din't show."

Phil moved one hand weakly. "I took the cliff trail."

"Of course," Killian said warmly. "It was right."

Phil looked at him through a haze of pain and

swirling weakness, and saw that Baxon had indeed followed, but not far enough to see him take Lester up the cliff, over the bridge, to the hunting and fishing shack where Jonathon had waited. He felt a pulse of excitement at how close it must have been. If Baxon had followed closer—and had seen Lester alive, fighting with him even as he tried to convince him to stay at the shack, and finally had to tie him up—it would have been over.

The door banged open and Baxon came in with Schwartz.

"Pop tole me," Baxon said. "I shoulda thought of it and gone to help him."

Phil laid his head back and almost smiled despite the pain. Baxon hadn't been helpful, or thoughtful, and that had saved him. The ruse was going to work. Jonathon could hold Lester a few days—maybe a week—and he would be well established in the gang. He could find out about the canyon, then—

He didn't think about it anymore. Grove and Schwartz, at a command from Killian, had gently but firmly pinned down his arms. And Baxon had leaned over him with a knife to probe for the shattered bullet fragment.

The knife cut into him and his body went stiff with agony, and he heard Killian say, "Take it as easy as you can. We want to get him well fast."

And then he passed out.

Chapter 10

It was hot. He was in bed, sticky with sweat. His shoulder hurt numbly, and his mouth had swollen dry. He wanted a drink of water.

Then he opened his eyes, and recognized the hotel room. There was a white water pitcher and a bowl on the dresser beside the bed. His gun belt had been folded and placed there too, along with his knife and wallet and money.

The sky outside the window looked like mid-afternoon. The wind was hot and suffocating.

He looked down at himself. He was naked to the waist. His shoulder had a bulky, clean bandage on it. It didn't hurt very much. He tried closing his fist and saw his fingers move as they should. He took a deep breath of relief.

"Testin'?" a familiar voice drawled.

He turned quickly to see Grove perched on a back-tilted chair on the other side of the bed. He was grinning and at ease, his spurred boots hiked up on the edge of the bed.

"Is there water in that pitcher?" Phil asked huskily.

Grove swung his legs to the floor, and his chair came upright. "Shore. Yuh want about a gallon?"

Phil smiled. "About."

Grove poured a glass and brought it to him. "Yuh lost blood, pardner."

Phil's throat drank the water greedily. He drained the glass and handed it back. "I guess I did."

"Feelin' okay?"

"I think so.—My arm's all right."

Grove felt his forehead with a cool hand. "Got mebbe a touch of fever. Nothin' serious."

Phil lay his head back on the pillow. "How long have I been out?"

Grove went back to his chair. "You come in las' night."

Phil relaxed. "Good." He thought of Jonathon holding Lester. He couldn't take too much time.

He asked, "Where is everybody?"

Grove motioned vaguely toward outdoors. "Here 'n there. Startin' to set up the deal for yuh to be sheriff."

"How is it going to work?"

"Ah better let Killian tell yuh."

Phil nodded. He would have to hold down the questions. He said, "I could use another shot of that water."

Grove moved lazily to the pitcher and filled the glass a second time. "Had some ruckus in town las' night."

"Oh?" Phil asked guardedly. "What about?"

Grove handed him the glass. "Lester. Cassie an' a couple of her men come in. She was plumb upset."

Phil's blood pumped sluggishly. "Did she think it was me?"

Grove grinned. "Uh-uh. She din't know what to think. They was jus' askin' around. Said somebody either hauled 'im off, or he rode off hisself, delirious."

"They heard the shots," Phil said.

"Yeah. But they don't seem to know rightly who to figger."

Phil stared at the ceiling, the thought of Cassie's anguish hurting. "They should have thought of me."

"Uh-uh," Grove smiled.

Phil looked at him questioningly.

"Killian mouthed it aroun' thet yuh're working for him. Tole ever'body yesterday yuh was ridin' to Dallas on a deal. They all jus' took it for granted yuh couldn't of been around." Grove cleared his throat. "Wal, Ah better go get the boss."

Phil nodded and watched Grove go to the door, glance back at him for an instant, then swing outside, closing the door behind him.

Then the door opened. It was Killian.

"Are you feeling better?" the dark-skinned man asked as he closed the door.

"Stiff," Phil said, "but better."

Killian sat on the edge of the bed. "Fever?"

"No. At least not much."

Killian's dark suit with his fancy white shirt was impeccable: spotlessly clean and newly pressed. He appeared to be untouched by the heat. His smooth-shaven face was dry.

"Ready to become our sheriff?" he asked with a smile.

"Anytime," Phil said, pulling himself to a sitting position.

Killian chuckled. "I really expected you to need a couple days to recover."

"No," Phil said. "I'm ready and eager."

"Good. We haven't been idle. Did Grove tell you you are supposed to be out of town?"

"Yes," Phil said. "When am I due back?"

Killian grinned. "If you feel able, tonight."

Phil leaned forward, tension trickling through his veins. "What happens?"

"The town council meets at the church at eight o'clock. You go there and tell them you want to help break my monoply on water. Then you come to the sheriff's old office—the council will give you the key—and set yourself up."

"Wait," Phil said. "How do we know they'll accept me?"

Killian lit a cigar. "Let us just say that they will have the right idea."

Phil frowned. "If you run the council—"

"I don't," Killian said. "One of the men on it—ah—does business with me. I believe he will lead a popular vote to hire you on a trial basis."

"They might not go along with it," Phil said. "Lots of people still hate me."

Killian blew smoke into the room. "Let me worry about that. I can assure you that you will have a trial." He looked at Phil narrowly, and Phil understood that he had the meeting rigged some way.

"All right," Phil agreed. "They give me a trial. Then what?"

"You clean up your office industriously," Killian said, smiling as if he were enjoying visions of it. "You wait until noon tomorrow. By that time everyone in town will know you are in office. Some of them may not like it, but I doubt that you will have any open opposition while the search for Lester is occupying them. That was a master stroke."

Phil didn't answer, so Killian went on:

"At noon you come to the Golden Eagle. You call me out. You tell me that I must lower the water rates drastically or you will kill me on the spot."

"Your men?" Phil asked.

"Unfortunately," Killian smiled, "on another mission."

Phil nodded.

"You threaten me," Killian went on, "and I attempt to draw my Derringer.—You knew I carried one, of course." He looked at Phil and nodded. "Of course you did.—At any rate, I start to draw it, and you hit me with your pistol.—I trust you won't hit too hard. You should bring blood, if you can do so without real injury."

He paused again, but Phil, amazed by the plan, didn't speak.

"Then," Killian said, "as I am at your feet—a dramatic spectacle certain to draw attention—you again demand lower water rates and less trouble from my men. You hold your gun on me as if you will kill me.—I accept bitterly."

For a long moment neither of them spoke again. Phil wiped sweat from his face and met Killian's mild gaze.

"And then," Phil said slowly, "they think I'm a hero—that you're afraid of me—and they really get behind me as sheriff."

"Precisely," Killian said.

Phil thought about it.

"If you are not able tonight," Killian said, "we can postpone it a few days. We want it to look realistic."

"I can do it now," Phil said quickly.

Killian stood nervously. "Good."

Phil hazarded, "With lower water rates and less

activity in town, I don't see how this can really help you."

Killian went to the window and looked out over the main street. "You know this town, Patterson. It can grow. With money moving into it, it can grow to become one of the biggest cities in Texas. It is directly on the route north for cattle."

He turned and looked at Phil. His eyes glittered. "Part of that money will come through me. We have things planned. I have a herd that rivals any in Texas not twenty miles from this hotel. It is hidden well. There are other operations we will enter. Guns. Whiskey. We can expand enormously and all the time appear to be legitimate. We can buy more in Redwater, and make it grow, and control the growth that will return dividends to our pockets."

Phil watched him as his eyes grew wider and he started breathing hard. Excitement made sweat pop out on his brow. He turned nervously and again looked out through the window.

"It can be ours," he said softly. "An empire!"

Phil swallowed. The lust for power—the vision of domination of the entire area—had transformed Killian into a man possessed by the craze for more and more—for everything he had ever dreamed of. This was no slick-talking criminal with ideas for making money on a large scale. This was a man caught up in a lust so great Phil could hardly comprehend it.

Killian turned to him quickly. "I hope you can be ready tonight."

"I can," Phil said. "I'll be there."

Killian puffed on his cigar, and the light slowly dulled in his eyes. He became again the soft-talking man Phil had known.

"Excellent," he said easily. "Excellent."

Then he turned toward the door. "I will send Grove back with new clothes for you. Join me at the Golden Eagle when you're ready to eat."

Phil agreed numbly, and the door shut behind his new boss.

The afternoon slid past. Phil ate with Killian and they ran over the meeting, and how it would be handled. Phil was to stay at the saloon alone at a table, playing solitaire. Killian's man would bring up the sheriff proposal at the meeting and ramrod it through. Then they would come to the Golden Eagle, or send a messenger for Phil to come to them. They would make the proposal and he would accept after acting reluctant at first, and discussing it at length.

"After you are appointed," Killian said, "you should find a deputy. How about your brother?"

"He won't get in it," Phil said.

"He doesn't have to work for me," Killian said. "He can work for you. Everyone knows he is scrupulously honest. He can stay that way. You can be his boss, and pay him. He should make it look good, and help you."

Phil hesitated. It might be better for Jonathon to go along with it. That way they could keep in close contact without being suspected.

He said slowly, "I'll ask him and see what he has to say."

"Strictly as a regular deputy," Killian said. "You tell him nothing."

"If I did," Phil admitted, "he wouldn't help us."

Killian smiled. "Of course."

Soon afterward, Killian left to attend the council meeting. He always attended, so it wouldn't look strange.

Phil stayed at the table in the Golden Eagle and played a slow game of solitaire, then another. The place slowly came alive as the evening passed. Voices carried over the clink of glasses, the soft crack of cards being shuffled, the click of the gambling wheels. Men of all appearances—young, too young to shave, bearded cattlemen, a few silent Mexicans—appeared, a few at a time, to fill the hall that glowed under gleaming chandeliers. Bare-shouldered whores sidled from table to table, provoking raucous laughter and joking. And sometimes money changed hands and they disappeared for a while.

Phil flipped his cards slowly, his untouched glass of whiskey before him. Once he saw Baxon and Tub hurry from the back room and go outside, but he didn't think much about it. He imagined they had some errand for Killian.

Several times men glanced at him questioningly, and once a farmer from the valley came over and smiled blearily and said it must have been wild in Dallas. The rest of the time Phil was left alone.

He kept thinking about Jonathon and Lester, and Cassie, too, but he kept dismissing them from his mind. It was a chance, but the whole thing was a chance. Jonathon could hold Lester. There was very little chance of anyone finding the shack without specifically searching for it.

Then, about the time he had begun to expect the council to arrive, the door swung open, and it was Jonathon.

His white face shone as he looked hurriedly

around the room and finally spotted Phil. He started over.

Phil didn't move or give any sign, but a pulse thudded in his temples.

There was trouble. Jonathon's pallid face, wild eyes and dusty clothes told him that.

It had to be Lester.

It was. Jonathon sat down and blew hard. "Phil," he said huskily, whispering. "Lester's gone!"

Chapter 11

PHIL BLINKED. The information sank into him slowly, spreading with cold fingers. Jonathon sank his sweaty face in his hands for a moment, then looked up again. He was white and exhausted. Phil thought of Killian. Had they found Lester?

"I went for some stuff," Jonathon said breathlessly. "I come back and he was gone."

"Did you have him tied?" Phil rapped.

"Yeah. He got untied. I don't know how."

"Had there been a fight? Could someone have untied him?"

Jonathon breathed deep. "Hell, Phil, I don't know. I didn't see anything. He left on foot—I tracked him a ways but then I couldn't see no more."

"Toward town?"

"You mean was he comin' toward town?—Yeah. Right at it."

"How long ago?"

"Half hour—maybe forty-five minutes."

"He might have been gone longer," Phil said, thinking aloud.

"I was gone over an hour," Jonathon said nervously.

Phil looked around the brawling room. None of

Killian's men were around.

"You didn't get him convinced why we had to hold him," he said.

Jonathon ran his hands through his hair. "I thought I did.—I guess I didn't.—Geez, he's on his way here, he might be here anytime!"

Phil gritted his teeth. "I can't go with you to hunt for him. I have to go to the council meeting quick."

Jonathon stood. "You want I should go out by the wells and watch?"

"You'd better," Phil decided. "If he isn't here pretty soon, you can figure he's either gotten through or changed his mind. Come back if he isn't there within forty minutes."

"Where'll you be?"

Phil thought a moment. "Here or at the council or at the hotel."

"What're you gonna *do?*"

Phil lit a cigarette and inhaled deeply. "I can't do anything but play it out. Maybe you'll catch Lester before Killian's bunch does."

"What if they get him first?"

"Then I start shooting," Phil clipped. "I can't give it away on a chance. We have to wait and hope we can get Lester before they do."

Jonathon stood stock-still, swaying on his feet.

"Get going," Phil hissed.

Jonathon headed for the door.

Phil stared at the table top and tried to think. If Lester had gotten loose and was headed for him, Jonathon probably would intercept him. If Killian's people had stumbled onto the cabin—Baxon had been still suspicious, perhaps, after hearing the gunshots—then Lester was already dead and he could count on action fast.

Or maybe Lester was free, but wouldn't show himself. If he did that, if he went home, the council meeting could go according to schedule.

He looked at the clock on the wall and realized that it was time to go to the council meeting.

He stood and walked to the door of the saloon. With a glance back, he shoved the door open and went out onto the dark board sidewalk.

There were horses in the dimness at the hitching rail, and people in the street. After the brightness of inside he could not see clearly and he stood beside the door as his eyes adjusted. The street was normal, men walking back and forth, talking, a rider coming in wearily drooping in his saddle, three men standing nearby talking in low tones. Phil didn't recognize any of them. His eyes opened to the dimmer light and when he could clearly make out the faces of the men nearby, he turned and started slowly down the sidewalk toward the church.

The church's windows glowed yellow with the lights of the meeting inside. A quick glance told him that there was no one outside the doors there, and he concentrated on the side street as he approached it. If Killian's men had gotten to Lester, it would be a good place for an ambush. It would be Baxon, maybe, or Tub. With a knife.

He kept moving at the same pace, five steps—then four—from the intersection. He couldn't see around it. He stepped into the street so no one could attack from directly around the corner with out warning. His nerves began to tingle as he took another step, another, and got to the intersection.

He looked down the darkened side street. It was empty.

He breathed deeply and strode on across it, nearing the church. The cool air smelled of dust and horses. His shirt clung to his back, wet with sweat. The sounds of the saloons racketed into the night air: men's hoarse voices and the clink of glasses, the shuffling of feet and coarse laughter. The buildings along the street in this block nearest the church were stores and sheds. They lurked black in the gloom of evening. Phil licked dry lips and almost wished it was in the open. He was fighting ghosts. He couldn't know if they had discovered him or not.

He walked up to the church door. It was white-painted and sturdy. A memory of going to church here touched his mind as he swung the door back to step inside.

The other doors of the vestibule were pulled back. The council was in meeting. At a low board-table sat five men under two glaring kerosene lanterns. They had papers in front of them and were talking. They stopped and looked up as he entered, as did a half-dozen spectators. Two of the spectators were half-drunken cowboys. Two were old people, evidently man and wife, gray-haired and thin. Another was a solemn-looking young man in a black coat, perhaps the minister. The other was Killian.

Phil knew two of the council members. The center one, apparently the chairman, was Fred Zinc, a stiff-suited cattleman with gnarled hands holding a scrap of official-looking paper. On the left end was Bert Livezey, the thin-faced, ascetic shopkeeper who had been a founder of Redwater.

Phil stepped into the room. He looked sharply at Killian, but found no sign of distrust.

"Phil Patterson," Zinc said with no emotion. "What brings you here? I heard you were in town."

Not hesitating, Phil walked up the aisle to the table. "I'm looking for a job. I think you have one."

The men glanced at each other quickly, and Zinc smiled faintly, caustically. "We hadn't advertised, Phil."

Phil met his gaze directly. "I want to be sheriff."

Zinc didn't change expression. "You're kinda late applyin', ain't you, Phil?"

Phil flushed. "I just got back."

He fought the impulse to look at Killian. One good look might tell him if Killian knew about Lester now, if Lester had been seen—

Livezey said, "We aren't looking for a new law man."

"Maybe you're not," Phil said. "But I'm applying."

"What do you feel you can gain?"

"Better water rates, for one thing."

Zinc's hands froze on the paper they held. No one spoke. Zinc looked toward Killian, then back at Phil. Livezey's cough sounded loud in the silent room.

Zinc cleared his throat. "You know—that is—Mister Killian is here with us, Phil, and he—"

"I know," Phil rapped, playing the part.

Zinc flicked a glance at Killian, then away again. "You might be thinking you can bite off more'n you can chew."

"Try me," Phil said.

Zinc looked at Livezey.

Livezey avoided Phil's gaze. "Personally, I think Phil has done enough in Redwater. I don't want him for sheriff."

Another man leaned forward to look down the table. "But if he can do what he says—if he'll—"

Livezey broke in, "Seems strange for you to be wantin' ruckus with Killian here, Frank."

Frank's eyes wavered for a moment—a tip that he was the one Killian controlled. Then he met his council member's eyes. "Maybe this is a real man I see here in front of us." His voice rang out sharply. "If he is, maybe he can do something good for this town."

"You caught us off our guard." Zinc muttered, reaching for a sack of tobacco. "Yes sir, caught us off guard."

The one called Frank leaned forward. "I think we ought to discuss it right now."

Zinc leaned back, concentrating on rolling a cigarette. "Well—"

"We ought to have Patterson leave, and discuss it," Frank persisted.

Zinc breathed heavily. He looked up at Phil. "I guess we'll take your offer under consideration. Now if you'll leave—and you too, Killian—we can get on with the Executive session."

Killian's voice sounded: "I have a right to listen."

Zinc looked at him mildly. "Executive session, Mister Killian. No spectators."

Killian glared at him—a good act, Phil thought—and turned on his heel to stride to the back of the room.

Zinc said to Phil, "Be around."

Phil nodded and turned.

Outside, in the darkness again, he almost ran into Killian.

"Go to your hotel," Killian snapped, moving away from him fast.

Phil hesitated, watching him disappear in the darkness. The others were coming out behind him.

They were talking in hushed, excited tones. The old man said, "By dern, if he can fix that Killian—" Then he was shushed by his wife.

Phil started slowly down the street. Why his hotel? For a moment there was worry.

But why not? he thought. Killian would go to the Golden Eagle. It wouldn't look right for both of them to be in the same place. The hotel was the place for him to be—they could find him there easily, and he wouldn't be near Killian.

He stretched his stride toward the ordered place. Maybe everything would go all right yet. Maybe Jonathon would intercept Lester, or maybe Lester was convinced, and was heading south, out of town. Maybe Lester just didn't like being held, but would go along with it.

Still, Phil thought as he stepped up onto the sidewalk and neared the hotel, it would have been a lot easier if Lester hadn't escaped. If Lester got to town and *they* saw him—

He let the thought go unfinished as he opened the hotel door and walked across the bright lobby. Men looked up as he passed, but he ignored them. He wished he knew how Jonathon was doing. So much depended on Lester now. Lester had to be found.

He mounted the steps to his room. Probably they would talk about it in the council meeting for an hour. Jonathon would be back. If Lester hadn't been seen, they'd better check the Michaels home. He might have gone there. They had to find him fast and stop this guessing, this going along with the plan not knowing whether it was all right or a slick trap.

He opened the door of his room. He stepped inside and fumbled for the lamp. He took out a match, struck it, and touched it to the strong-smelling wick. It came to life, filling the room with soft, yellow light. He put the lamp on the table—

"Jesus," he muttered.

On the floor, in a thick, black pool of blood, lay Lester Michaels. His head had been bashed in with an ax that lay beside his body.

Sickened, Phil stared at the body. It was covered with dirt and sand. It had been dragged a long distance. Lester must have been killed instantly. The ax had hit him in the face and there wasn't much left.

Phil flipped out his .44 and spun the cylinder. Full. He turned the gun over in his hand. It looked beat-up, with no front sight or trigger. It was worn white along the barrel where it leaped from the holster. It was heavy and well-balanced, a good gun. It seemed to nestle into his hand.

He dropped it into the holster, swung his arm loosely, and drew. His shoulder shot pain, but the gun came up ready in a smooth, effortless motion. He dropped it into the holster again and drew again. The only sound was a slight slap as his hand hit the butt and jerked it free.

It was clear that they knew. They had found Lester or he wouldn't be dead. Now it was in the open, and Phil felt relieved. The issue was clear: kill them.

As he turned toward the door, he felt an unaccustomed pulse of hatred. He was going to enjoy it.

He opened the door. The hallway was empty. He closed the door, turned the key in the lock and slipped the key into his shirt pocket. He walked down the hall to the stairs and looked down into the lobby.

Nothing had changed. The clerk stood behind the reception desk, idly turning the pages of an old newspaper. A drummer, with his satchel of wares at his side, sat slumped in an overstuffed red leather chair by the front window. Another man, wearing a frayed vest and coat and black stovepipe hat, slouched in another chair on the far side. His eyes were closed. Beyond the windows of the street was utter darkness.

Phil watched silently, unmoving.

Why had Killian told him to come back here, where he knew the body would provide warning? Why hadn't he ordered Schwartz or Baxon or Grove to do the job with a rifle or knife in the street?

The question made him remain motionless at the top of the stairs. There had to be an answer, and he couldn't come up with it. Sweat ran down his throat and onto his chest. His ears strained for sound, but the town seemed silent. The smells of stale tobacco and dust filled the air. The stairs creaked as he moved slightly, shifting his weight.

Maybe, he thought, Killian knew he would act when he found Lester's body. Maybe Killian had some of them outside in the dark so they could be sure, in position and hidden from his brightness-stunned eyes, when he rushed outside after finding Lester.

He turned and stared down the hall. At the far end was a door that led onto the balcony.

He pivoted and strode down the hall to the door. His breath came fast as he stood by it a moment, listening. His heart thudded loud. He tried the doorknob. It turned under his hand. He swung the door open.

Nothing happened. The door swung back on a

gentle breeze, and he heard street noises—the clopping of a horse's hooves, laughter from a saloon, the rumble of voices.

The balcony was empty. He looked down on the street. A man on horseback rode slowly by, head bowed. Three or four men swaggered out of a bar. One of them whooped and fell down the steps. The others roared and bent over to help him up. He cursed and refused their help. He climbed to his feet and staggered after them toward another saloon. The door opened brightly, then closed behind them.

A half-moon beamed wanly over the blackened roofs of buildings. The wind caught Phil's shirt and pressed it against his damp chest. He swung his leg over the balcony railing, looked down to the street for an instant, and dropped.

He hit hard. The shock numbed his legs. He climbed to his feet and shot a glance around. The board sidewalk was vacant. Inside the hotel, in the bright light of the lobby, two men were talking with the clerk, who was pointing upstairs. The clerk's face was animated as he explained something and smiled obsequiously. The men turned toward the stairs.

The first was Zinc. The other was Frank.

Phil stifled a curse. Of course! Killian would let them find Lester's body in his room. Then Phil Patterson would be an outlaw here, and would have to die. Killian could turn the surprise of Lester's arrival into an advantage; killing Phil would be a civic duty.

For a moment Phil vacillated. He could either go after Killian at once, or fight for extra time with the council.

He didn't know why he decided, but he turned

and gauged the distance back to the balcony. He crouched, then sprang. His hands caught the edge of the roof and he hauled hard. Something ripped in his shoulder and he felt hot blood run down his arm. He pulled himself up, caught a knee on the edge, and clambered back onto the balcony.

He wheeled into the hall through the open door. He slammed the door and raced down the hall to his room. Jerking the key from his shirt-pocket, he struck it in the lock.

"Mister Patterson!" a voice—Zinc's—called from the stairs.

Phil looked. They had surmounted the steps and walked toward him down the hall. Zinc grinned broadly.

"Were you getting impatient?" he asked.

"No," Phil said. "I mean yes—I was coming over."

Zinc extended his hand. "No need. Let's go inside and talk."

The key had turned under Phil's hand, but he held the door with the other. "What did you decide?" he asked huskily.

Zinc looked at the door. "Let's go inside. Confidential."

"No," Phil said. He added quickly, "I have some —private papers."

Zinc stared at him questioningly. Phil felt sweat roll down his face. He met Zinc's gaze.

Zinc dropped his eyes and shrugged. "Okay.— We were surprised by your offer, of course, Phil, but we don't see why we can't give you a trial. Of course there are some conditions."

He paused and again looked at the door. "We'll haf to talk in private."

Phil glanced at Zinc's companion. "How about a

cup of coffee? We can get a table where no one could listen."

Zinc looked at him narrowly. "You seem awful nervous about us goin' in there, Phil."

"It's my business," Phil rapped. His hand strayed near his gun.

Zinc saw the movement. Color drained from his face. "I wasn't questioning you, Phil. Take it easy. I was just—curious."

"Let's have that coffee," Frank said gruffly.

"Right," Zinc said gratefully.

Phil turned to lock the door of the room. "I'll just—"

He stopped.

A stream of blood had trickled under the door into the hall.

He wasn't able to hide his glance fast enough. Zinc's eyes went to the floor where he had looked. Zinc's eyes widened and he started to look up at Phil.

Phil's gun came out smoothly. He backed away from the door. The door swung open gently on the gory scene within. The men didn't look. They stared into the barrel of Phil's gun.

"Stand right there," Phil grated.

They froze.

He backed away from them toward the door. His mind raced. Get into the street and toward the Golden Eagle—

A small hard object slammed into his back.

"Don't move," Grove's soft voice purred in his ear. "I'll kill you."

Chapter 12

PHIL stood frozen, gun still in hand. The hard barrel of Grove's revolver gouged into the small of his back. It prodded deeper.

"Drop it," Grove rapped.

Phil hesitated.

He heard the hammer of Grove's gun slide back. "I'll have to kill yuh," Grove said softly.

With a muttered oath Phil dropped his gun. It clattered to the wooden floor.

"Pick it up," Grove snapped at the other men.

Zinc hurried forward and scooped up the weapon. He stared at Phil unbelievingly.

"I voted for you in that meeting," he said huskily. "They said you was a killer, and I said you wasn't."

"I didn't kill him," Phil said, knowing it wouldn't be believed. "I just found him there."

Grove still held the gun in his back. "Guess it was lucky I come up to see my girl, gen'lemen."

Phil could tell Killian's man hadn't been warned. His eyes rolled nervously as he tried to figure out what to say. His mouth opened and closed without making a sound.

"Ya'all want to take 'im to jail?" Grove asked gently. He hadn't moved where Phil might have a chance to get at him. He was too smart for any ordinary trick. That was why Killian had assigned the job to him, Phil thought bitterly.

Zinc wiped his face with a red bandana. "Yes. We'd better take him to jail."

"I'll take 'im in for yuh," Grove said.

"Let's go," Zinc said, turning.

As the man turned, his hand holding Phil's gun swung within three feet of Phil's body.

Phil's body acted without thought. He slammed his elbow back into Grove's stomach, Grove grunted and doubled over. Phil leaped out and grabbed the gun from Zinc's hand. He sprawled as he got hold of it. He rolled over and snapped a shot at Grove just as Grove's gun went off. Grove's bullet smashed into the wall an inch from Phil's head. Then Grove was hurtled back by the impact of Phil's shot. He doubled up and the gun tipped out of his hand.

Phil didn't see more. He was on his feet. He slammed past Zinc and Frank and threw himself out onto the balcony. Without looking he vaulted the railing and hit in the dusty street. Someone was there beside a horse. He yelled. Phil came to his feet and started running blindly.

The roar of a shotgun split the night. Missiles tore the air around Phil's legs. He leaped onto the board sidewalk across the street from the hotel and cut around a corner. He heard shouts and gunfire. He felt nothing. His breath tore from his lungs. Storefronts blurred past his eyes. His boots pounded on the planks. Ahead he saw the yawning open door of a barn.

A bullet sang ugly past his head and splattered wood on his shoulders. He heard the shot. The door of the barn was beside him. He cut sharply into the blackness.

There was straw underfoot. No light. Horses trampled nervously. Phil's shoulder was matted and heavy with blood—the wound had opened again. Yellow stars danced before his eyes. He heard them coming.

Plunging blindly toward the back of the barn, he ran directly into a post and bounced off. He came back to his feet and pivoted around it. He headed for the dim outline of a window in the black wall.

"He's in here!" a voice shouted hoarsely at the front door.

Phil clambered up bales of hay to the window. It was small, heavily framed, covered with cobwebs and filth. He stood precariously on the bales, lowered his head and threw himself against the window.

It gave away with a shattering impact. Glass cut hot into his face and neck as he fell through. He turned over in the air and hit on his back. He still had the gun. Someone inside shot at the sound.

Sobbing for breath, Phil came to his feet again and looked around. He was in an alley. To his left were lights. To his right was blackness. He raced to his right, stumbling and almost falling over a crate. His eyes were open but he couldn't see a thing. He ran straight ahead and saw a glimmer of yellow ahead and aimed toward it. They were behind him again, in chase. He heard their shouts.

He pounded around a bend in the alley—and skidded to a halt.

The light he had seen came from a high window —the only one. To his left was the blank wall of a barn. The building at his right had no door or window into the alley that he could reach. Straight ahead was a high, smooth board fence. Dead end.

Cursing, he ran and leaped for the top of the fence. His chest smashed against the solid wood and his breath went out of his body. His reaching fingers missed the top and he fell heavily.

He heard them coming, running and yelling. Again he shot a glance around. There had to be a way out—

There wasn't. The smooth dirt was littered with the debris of the town, old tobacco sacks, paper, broken glass. The buildings on both sides were too high. The fence was solid and built right into the buildings.

He stepped quickly into the darkest corner. Panting, he faced the curve around which they would have to come.

The footsteps pounded nearer. He raised his gun.

"He went around here!" a man cried shrilly.

The man whirled around the corner into the dim light. He had a shotgun.

Phil fired and the man spun around twice. His shotgun stood on end for an instant as he fell limp. Two more men raced around the corner. Phil's gun leaped alive in his hand and the orange flame lanced out at them. One fell with a hoarse shout. The other fell over backward getting back behind the building.

Lights blazed around the corner, throwing confused shadows.

"He's right around there!" a man shouted. "He kill Jake?"

"He's layin' there—let's rush 'im!"

"All at once—"

The voices clattered together.

Phil gritted his teeth and looked over the barrel of his gun. His body trembled. He couldn't see clearly. In a second they would charge. He didn't recognize the voices. Most of them probably didn't even know who they were chasing, or why. This wasn't Killian now; it was the town. They had seen the chase and joined it. When they found out who they were chasing, and about Lester's death, they would be angry. Now they were just excited, afraid, ready for a fight because one was here.

He crouched lower against the fence. The light had gotten brighter. The men yelled at each other, steeling each other for the charge. He lifted the hammer on his gun. Four shots.

Something hit the fence at his back—somebody on the other side. He turned, raising the gun.

He saw something—somebody—come over the fence. The man hit his shoulders with crushing weight. A hot flame danced against the side of his head and he didn't know anything more.

His head was breaking apart. He knew it had been hurting for a long time, but now he moved, rolling on a hard, cold surface, and he tasted hot saltiness in his mouth. He swallowed. It made him lurch inside and almost throw up. He heard voices. They were talking about him because he heard one of the voices use his name. His head rocketed pain that split across the middle and throbbed like his skull would burst. He groaned and squeezed his temples.

A voice—Grove's—said quite clearly, "He's 'bout out of it now."

Phil's eyes opened. The light shocked them, hurting worse. He squinted against the pain.

Killian and Grove sat at a beat-up roll-top desk

near him. He was on the floor of a barren room with sod walls. He recognized it instantly. The jail.

Eyes still dazzled by the light of the lantern on the desk, he stared at his captors.

Grove smiled. "Tub shore hit 'im a lick."

Killian looked down at him unsmiling. "You're awake."

Phil licked bloody lips and felt sick again. He didn't answer. He tried to remember. The council meeting—the—Lester—

Then he remembered all of it. It must have been Tub who came over the fence at him.

He touched the side of his head. His fingers burned against raw flesh. He felt the smoothness of bone. The side of his face had been laid open by the blow. It was still bleeding freely. The floor was soggy around him.

A knife-like pain shot through his skull and everything blurred. So they had gotten him to jail, and now he was a murderer. Zinc was respected. He would tell them all that Phil Patterson had killed Lester Michaels—"I saw it myself, the body in his room—No, with an ax. Right in the face. Terrible."

First old man Michaels, they'd say, and now his kid.

Killian showed no emotion. His immaculate dark suit was untouched by the dustiness of the room. A slender cigar trailed smoke from one of his ringed hands. The lantern-light gleamed off his oily black hair.

"Grove is Redwater's new sheriff," he said calmly.

Phil glanced at Grove and saw the dull star on his shirt-front.

"I should say it has worked out quite well," Killian said.

Grove's face split in a lazy grin. "Always wanted to be a law man."

"You killed Lester," Phil said huskily.

Killian puffed the cigar. "The body was found in your room, Patterson. The consensus seems to be—"

"You killed him," Phil repeated through gritted teeth.

Killian stifled a polite yawn with the back of his hand. "How long do you suppose it will take them, Grove?"

"I dunno," Grove said. "Not much more."

Killian got up and walked to the door, and opened it. Noise came from the street outside—the distant sound of men's angry voices.

Killian closed the door. "It will not be long."

Phil glared at him.

"The lynch mob," Killian smiled. "We brought you here in custody. You are to stand trial. Of course if the people decide to lynch you, there isn't a lot the two of us can do about it."

Killian sat down again. Phil stared around the bare walls of the room.

"If you are looking for escape," Killian said, "there isn't any. Your brother has been taken care of."

Phil lurched. "Jonathon?"

Killian studied his cigar. "Nothing violent. But we thought it might be better if he were spared the sight of seeing you hang."

"I won't hang," Phil gritted.

Killian chuckled. "You'll hang."

Phil looked at Grove. Grove's expression was

emotionless. Their eyes met. Grove was a professional with a job. His eyes, without feeling, said that clearly. Phil understood. If their roles had been reversed, he might have felt the same.

Phil looked down and tried to think. They had dragged him from the alley. He was caked with dust and manure. His head and shoulder pulsed with agony. His gun was gone. If Jonathon was captive, there was no one who might help. The others who had gone together to hire him?—He rejected it. They hadn't shown yet. They couldn't help if a lynch mob was gathering. Only guns stopped a lynch mob.

He shuddered despite himself. He had seen a lynching. He had been too late to see the rope hauled up, but he had gotten there as the body hung free, the legs still kicking convulsively, the black face contorting in the rage to live, the blood bursting from the nostrils—

It wouldn't do any good to think of that. If they were coming for him, he had to get free first.

He gauged the distance between the desk and his position. Too far. Grove's gun, seemingly held laxly, didn't waver from his head. A move and he was dead.

Some other way, he thought numbly. There had to be some other way.

Killian said, "You almost had us, Patterson."

Phil met his dark-eyed gaze.

"You almost had us," Killian repeated thoughtfully. "Sheer luck.—If Schwartz hadn't been in the Queen Bee when Michaels went in there, you might have gotten him again first and we could have gone on and hung ourselves."

"Was it Schwartz who killed him?" Phil rapped.

"No," Killian said, rounding his mouth with the

word. "Tub got that honor."

Phil didn't say anything. His anger strangled him.

Killian said, "Perhaps my mistake was in underestimating you. I thought men like you and Brewster were good only in the middle of the street, facing each other."

Phil hardly listened. It seemed the sound of the crowd was growing in volume. They weren't approaching yet, but he could hear the dull roar of angry voices through the closed door. If they came for him—

Killian said, "Brewster wanted to kill you himself. But I think this is much more satisfactory. Grove and I shall fight to defend your right to a trial. Then they will overcome us and lynch you. You will be dead, and they will have guilt feelings. As your defenders, we will be honorable. Grove will be sheriff. He can be a fairly good sheriff."

"I should have killed you when I had a chance," Phil clipped.

Killian stood. "You didn't." He moved suddenly and his foot crashed into Phil's side, toppling him in a purple shot of pain.

"You didn't do this alone," Killian snapped. "Who hired you?"

Phil lay on his side, gasping for breath. He couldn't answer.

Killian's boot slammed solidly against his spine. Fire lanced up his back and down into his legs and he bit his tongue to keep from crying out.

"Filth," Killian hissed. "Who hired you?"

"I came home," Phil gasped. "I—"

Killian spat on his face. "You don't have time for lies."

Phil tried to roll over. Again Killian's boot

cracked into his spine. It numbed him all over. He fell flat on his face and couldn't move. Hot blood ran into his mouth. He couldn't even tense for another blow.

"It will not be long," Killian said harshly.

Phil fought to drag air into his tortured lungs. The rough boards of the floor cut into his face. His arms and legs went hot as feeling crept back into them. If he could have moved he would have hurled himself upward. He told his arms and legs to move, but they didn't respond.

Killian's voice sounded farther away: "Perhaps you could escape the lynching if you told us."

The words shocked Phil nearer consciousness.

"There might be an escape if we knew who had hired you," Killian said, his voice soft again.

Phil heaved himself up to a sitting position. He reeled and almost fell. Then he caught himself and shook things into focus.

"Escape to be shot in the back?" he muttered.

"If they hired you," Killian said through a buzzing noise that was in Phil's ears, "they might hire others. Tell us who they are and you can ride."

Phil felt an insane impulse to laugh. "I don't even know."

"You'll die," Killian rapped. "If you—"

"Bastard," Phil gritted. "I wouldn't tell you."

Killian's face darkened. He stood. He reached inside his coat and a tiny pistol—a Derringer—appeared in his hand. He leveled it at Phil. "I'll kill you now," he hissed.

Phil stared into the gun barrel without flinching.

"Listen, boss," Grove said quickly.

Killian hesitated.

The crowd noise had gotten louder, uglier, throbbing with latent violence. But that wasn't what had stopped Killian.

A horse had pounded up to the door. They all looked.

The door swung open. It was Cassie, wild-eyed, cheeks flushed from a hard ride in the wind. Dust coated the bright red dress she wore, and its full skirt billowed as she whirled into the room and slammed the door behind her. She turned angry-eyed on Killian.

"They're going to lynch him!" she cried.

Killian rose, hiding the gun neatly. "Cassie, my dear—"

Cassie turned to Phil. With a sob she fell to her knees beside him. "I know you didn't do it," she choked, her wet face against his. She was sobbing and her breast pressed against him. "They told me —it had to be them, but I can't find Jonathon—the mob down there—"

Killian was gently drawing her to her feet. For a split-second she slumped against Killian, and he started to put his arm around her.

Face crimson, she pulled away. Her arm blurred and her hand cracked against his face. He actually staggered.

"Don't *touch* me!" she cried. "You did it!"

Killian held his cheek. His eyes burned hot, but he held himself in check. "This man did it, Cassie, and—"

"Phil didn't come back alone," she said softly, her voice going almost to a whisper. "Do you know how many people got together to get him here?" She bent, crouching, her eyes shooting sparks of anger.

"Were you among them?" Killian asked with a new tone.

She tossed her head. "I didn't know—I just

found out. But there were lots of them. They know Phil didn't do this!"

Killian inclined his head and listened for a moment, then smiled. "Do you suppose you can convince the men who are coming?"

Cassie's face went the color of chalk.

Phil's ears strained at the rumbling of the crowd. It grew louder. He heard individual voices now, curses and shrill shouts. He heard the scuffling of feet. They were on the move.

Killian wiped his cheek gently with a piece of white linen. "You should leave, Cassie. This will not be pretty."

Cassie stared down at Phil. He met her gaze. A lump filled his throat at the sight of her. Her face was streaked with tears. She was white. Her hands trembled. He thought she might faint. She looked suddenly small and fragile and helpless—still a very young woman, one who had lost her dream, her husband, her father and brother. She looked suddenly defeated.

The men's voices grew louder. The mob sounded like a growing animal.

"Go," Phil said huskily. "Get out, Cassie."

"I can't!" she wept. "They'll kill you!"

"Get out," Phil rapped. "They'll kill you too if you don't go!"

Cassie hesitated another moment. Despite the pain and confusion, Phil felt a rush of love for her. She stood straight and fine and afraid, not knowing what to do. All he could think of was getting her clear of what might happen.

"In the name of God," he cried. "Get out fast!"

She turned without a word and disappeared through the door.

Killian sprang to the door behind her. He swung

it open. Phil saw Cassie, on horseback, leap away. Beyond her was the black mass of the mob. Men swinging lanterns and ropes led the way. Behind them were others. Pitchforks and shovels stuck up out of the welter of movement. There were thirty or forty of them. They crushed forward inexorably.

Killian stood in the open door. He held up his hands. "Wait!"

The men paused for a moment. Lanterns threw yellow light on frenzied, drunken faces.

"What d'ya want?" one man raged. "Get outta the way!"

"Yeah!" a dozen voices took up the cry. "Get outta the way!"

The mob surged forward.

"This man must have a trial!" Killian shouted.

"Did he give Michaels a trial?" roared a big, rope-armed man in front.

With a thunderous shout they surged forward again, not ten feet from the door.

Killian turned, smiling, and motioned to Grove.

The professional gunman went to the door. He had his gun in hand.

The men slowed and looked up at him.

"Outta the way!" one of the crowd yelled hoarsely. "We want 'im!"

"I'm acting sheriff," Grove drawled, his voice a sharp contrast to the vivid scene. "Patterson ain't gonna be lynched."

"The hell he ain't!" another man screamed, hurling a lantern.

The glass dome burst against the door of the jail and Grove reeled back. Flame gushed up on the floor as the men shoved forward.

"Too anxious—" Grove muttered, striding toward the back.

But then Phil didn't hear anymore. He was on his feet and diving at Grove's gun.

He wasn't quick enough. Just as the first men bolted through the door, Grove swung the gun in a short, vicious arc. It connected solidly on Phil's head and he slumped to the floor.

Instantly he was in a mass of legs all around him, and he was getting stepped on in the confusion. He didn't lose consciousness. A gun went off—once—twice—and then a dozen hands grabbed him and jerked him up. Still too stunned to fight, he was thrown into the air and held up by a mass of strong arms. His bad shoulder was cracked sharply against the door jamb as they hurtled him out into the night on their shoulders. He was helpless.

Up on their shoulders with a dozen hands holding him he was carried into the middle of the street. Lanterns and torches spun in crazy pinwheels. Shouting voices roared through the buzzing pain in his head and he knew Tub was with them, right in the middle of it. Tub had a hand fisted into his shirt. Phil knew more by instinct than mentality that they were carrying him south, toward the cottonwoods. That was the place for hanging.

He fought at the hands holding him. If he could break loose for just an instant he could run. He kicked out as hard as he could. They dropped his legs and someone shouted. His shirt tore away and he fell hard in a mass of moving legs. Someone stepped on him. He tried to come to his feet. A heavy weight hit his shoulders. Something metallic crashed into his mouth and he saw bright yellow of a lantern. He choked on blood and broken teeth. His legs were swooped out from under him and they had him up again, more hands than ever, almost upside down. His face roared with pain that shot up into the sockets of his eyes. He was blinded. He sobbed for air. Hands grasped his bare flesh, fingernails tearing like fish hooks into his skin. The garish lights of the Golden Eagle blurred past as he found he could see vaguely. Figures moved against the lights with nightmare unreality. He coughed and tasted vomit with the blood.

He had never stopped fighting. He was fighting instinctively. He tore one of his hands free and shot it stiff-fingered into someone's face. A man howled in pain and a grasp loosened on his arm. He swung his arm, his left one, up over his body and down on top of somebody's head. Then hands shot up and pulled him down and he half rolled over with his face down. A fleshy fist caught his chin with a glancing blow.

He fell limp. Something whispered that they might relax if they thought he was unconscious. He let every muscle go limp, head hanging, and they rolled onward unslowed.

"He passed out!" someone roared in his ear.

A dozen voices yelled replies. One shouted hoarsely, "We'll get 'im awake for the hangin'." It was shouted gleefully, hysterically. Men roared laughter and cursed and a lantern hit the ground and burst into flame, and was left behind, a puddle of light in darkness.

They were at the edge of town. The lights started to fall back and the mob was in darkness. It couldn't be over a hundred yards to the trees. Phil panicked and shot his arms and legs out rigid. Cursing, he threw himself against the hands that held him. They squeezed harder and someone shouted, his hot breath hitting Phil's face. Phil tore loose from one and got pulled around, half sitting up. He swung with all his strength and connected solidly in a man's face. Then he saw the shovel swing in a flat arc but he couldn't duck. It glanced off the side of his head. Oddly, he didn't feel it. But he fell over backward and was back in the crushing grip of hands.

The stench of kerosene and sweat stung his nostrils. His body burned. His mouth was slippery with blood. A blurred mass of bodies and spinning lights raced before his eyes as he turned over, bouncing along on their hands above their heads, and he saw for an instant the cool black sky. The raucous shouts of the mob smoothed into a deep-throated din in his ears.

Suddenly only three or four men held him; they let go and he fell.

Looking up he saw them all around him in a circle. Their faces glowed yellow with the dancing excitement of death. Tub was nearest. His arm swung lazily and a coil of rope sailed out of the lantern light. Then the end fell back a foot from where Phil lay.

"We ain't got a horse!" someone shrilled.

"Get a horse!" someone else cried.

"No!" Tub roared. "Haul 'im up!"

"Haul 'im up," a ghastly-faced kid yelled shrilly. "Make 'im last!"

Tub's face split into a leer. He stepped forward with the rope dangling in a noose from his right hand.

Phil spun on the ground and shot his legs into Tub's mid-section. Tub whooshed air and bent double. Phil came to his knees. Men scattered, a lantern fell. A gun in a holster. Phil leaped for it. His hands closed on it as he fell and the man started down under his weight and the gun tore free. Someone jumped toward Phil and he thumbed the hammer. The man's face blew up in a red spurt.

Phil rolled. He shot again into a mass of bodies. Someone shouted. He came to one knee and shot again. The gun roared and spat orange. A man fell.

But he was surrounded. A ton of weight crashed onto his back. He went forward under it. His face jammed into spit-wet sand. The gun tore from his doubled wrist. The weight bore down on his face, crushing him into the earth. They were all over him. His muscles screamed to act but he couldn't move. His body fought of its own volition, tearing against the weight that couldn't be budged. The weight crushed down and he was blacking out—

The weight came off. He knew it, but he couldn't move.

Hands hauled him to his feet. He collapsed and started to fall and they held hm. He couldn't see. His eyes were open and he couldn't see. His lungs bellowed. Hot life surged back through him, knives in his veins. He started to see again through a curtain of crimson.

The cool coil of the rope fell over his head and around his neck.

"Haul 'im up!" Tub's voice screamed in his ear.

Sticky saliva hit his face.

"Haul!" voices roared together.

The hands let go of him. He started to sag. The rope sang tight around his neck.

It caught at his Adam's apple. He gagged. It tightened. He tore at it with his hands. It dug deep into his throat. His breath shut off. It hauled up on him. He stretched. He thought his head would tear off his shoulders. His lungs spasmed and shut and he knew he was blacking out. He went to tip-toe, swaying, fighting the rope—then he was clear of the ground. He thought how strange it was that his neck should support his body. His hands peeled flesh from his neck, but the steel rope didn't budge. It was rock-like, knifing deep inside him. He wasn't breathing. He knew he couldn't last. He kicked out and the rope jerked harder, tearing something at the base of his skull. They were shouting, shrill man-shouts racketing through the thunder in his brain, and the hot fire of strangulation surged through him, blackness deeper than any he had ever known, his legs going limp—hang still, maybe it won't hurt, hang still and don't fight, the rumble of a waterfall in his ears and salty blood bursting out of his nostrils—it would be like that, it had to be—swaying, the pain exquisite through every fibre writhing for air and getting none, lungs fluttering, heart thudding huge in the chest.

Suddenly he fell.

The rope peeled from his neck. He retched. A gun was thrust into his hands. He held the gun up and squeezed the trigger with both hands and it went off. He squeezed the trigger again—again, his throat trying to shout words, nothing coming, and then he saw Jonathon pulling at him, trying to get him to his feet.

He staggered up. There was gunfire—winging flame and shots—all around him. He saw men on wheeling horses, firing. The mob had broken and fallen back. Bullets sang overhead. A horse almost stepped on him. Someone reached down and grabbed him under the armpits and heaved upward. He grabbed a saddle strap and helped, weakly. He got one leg over the horse and fell forward against the rider. The horse bolted.

He twisted his hands around saddle leather until he felt the straps cut deep into his wrists. Then in the whirling, pounding stride of the horse, he passed out.

Chapter 13

FRANK SULLIVAN, a big, beefy-faced rancher, sat facing Phil's cot in the living room of the Michaels ranch house. Behind Sullivan's broad back, outside, four men sat on the porch with rifles across their knees. Another man sat his horse fifty yards away, at the edge of the woods. Phil lay on the cot, swathed in homemade bandages. His face felt sticky from the salves on his cheeks and mouth. Both arms were bandaged to the forearm. They had smeared grease on his puffed throat. When he spoke it was in a rasping whisper. His words weren't clear because his front teeth were gone and his mouth was still seeping blood from the empty sockets. Whenever he moved his legs, pain shot the length of them and into his pelvis. Pulsing pains slanted through his head, but that was feeling better. His hair was matted and heavy.

Sullivan scratched his sandy-colored hair and turned shaggy-browed eyes to Phil's face. "You figger they'll hang in town and jus' wait us out?"

"I don't know," Phil rasped. He ran his tongue over the holes in his gums. "Killian can't leave if he has that cattle here. Maybe he'll just come after us."

Sullivan touched the gun stuck in his waist. "Not

now he knows we're done sitting on our haunches and watchin' 'im stick it to us."

Phil smiled bitterly. "There are lots of people in Redwater that want my blood."

"Yeah," Sullivan snorted. "They jus' damn well better not try anything, neither."

Phil turned to his side, biting his tongue to combat the pain. The lynching had brought his backers into the open. Sullivan and two of the others, Janakowski and O'Malley, had been in town. O'Malley had gone to get the others. They had gotten there to cut him down just in time. It had taken them a long time coming into the open against Killian, but now that they had moved they were all endowed with the same tight-lipped certainty of purpose that Sullivan showed now. They were ready to fight.

Phil said slowly, "Lots of people will believe I killed Lester. Grove is set up as sheriff. They might not like it, exactly, but they'll keep quiet. They want me worse than anybody."

"Well," Sullivan muttered darkly, "they ain't gettin' you."

"Maybe they don't plan to," Phil said. "They know we have to do the coming if we're going to do anything now. Killian's got things sewed up."

A rustle of taffeta announced that Cassie had come back from the well. Wan and taut-faced, she came through the door and to Phil's cot. Her dark-rimmed eyes swept up to meet his for an instant, then she unfolded one of the cool towels she carried. Her slender hands removed a towel from Phil's forehead and replaced it with the cool one. Her lips parted in concentration as she smoothed it on his brow. It felt good, soothing. Her breasts moved softly under the silken material of her simple blue dress.

"All right?" she asked huskily, so low he almost couldn't understand.

"Yes," he muttered, tight-lipped so she wouldn't see his mouth.

But even so a shadow of pain passed behind her eyes as she looked at him.

"Can I get you anything?" she asked.

He shook his head.

She stood, smoothing her dress, and sat in the chair beside Sullivan's. Her haunted eyes rested on Phil's face. Her slender hands twisted together nervously.

It was a new look, and Phil didn't know what it meant. He wished she wouldn't see him like this because he knew it hurt her, perhaps even sickened her. But he wanted her there. Through the night when he had been sick at his stomach it had been Cassie at his side with towels and the basin and water, wiping him off, holding the light and caring for him, her cool hands gently doing what was necessary while the men watched and obeyed her sharp commands. Then he had slept, and when he awakened and sat bolt upright, shaking, remembering the noose, she had been by his side, holding his shoulders with fierce strength, whispering that it was all right. He wanted her with him.

Sullivan said, "We was wonderin' what Killian's bunch will do now."

Cassie looked at him, but didn't say anything. Her eyes went outside, to the men with rifles.

"If they come out here," Sullivan snorted, "we'll bore hell out of 'em."

"I don't think they will," Phil said, fighting to speak normally.

"What, then?" Sullivan asked.

"Like I said," Phil replied. "We have to go to town to hurt them any."

Sullivan stared at his big-knuckled hands. Clearly he was wondering how it was going to turn out. "Well, we'll go in there soon enough," he said stubbornly.

"We still don't know where they've got the cattle," Phil said.

Sullivan's face flushed. "Damn the cows! I'm ready to clean them people out!"

Phil smiled despite the way it hurt his face. They were together now, all of them who had hired him. Nine of them were out there, fidgeting for a fight. More than Killian had or could count on. But none of them were pros like Grove or Brewster. Some of them had never even seen a man die.

He ticked them off in his mind, the people who had saved him: Sam Smith, Sullivan, O'Malley, Janakowski, Bill Bryan, Jack Garner, Fats Matheson, John Davis, John Eberhart. All cattlemen but Garner, and he was a retired farmer. Bryan the youngest, maybe 35. Family men. Right now maybe thinking of their kids and wives, wondering if Killian might do something to them.

That was the weakness. The families, the homes, the hard-earned land and cattle. Possessions. Loved ones. Things to lose.

Worry flickered across Phil's mind. Maybe they'd stay worked up a day, maybe two. But then they'd begin to think too much about the work not being done, the families alone, the cattle straying, the fences that needed mending, the chores. Killian wouldn't seem quite such a threat.

So it was clear. They had to act fast if they were to be together and have advantage.

He smiled inwardly at the thought of advantage.

Really they had none. Not against Brewster and Grove. Not even against Tub or Schwartz or Baxon. Killian still held the top cards. He still ran the town, and he had people believing Lester had been murdered by Phil Patterson. He might even be able to get deputies—cowboys and roughnecks that didn't have anything better to do—and outnumber those with Phil. Maybe that was what Killian and Grove were doing right now.

Urgency tugged at Phil's brain. Act fast. Hit them now or you won't be able to.

No one had said anything for a while. Sullivan slapped his leg impatiently. "Guess I'll go jaw with the boys."

Phil nodded and let him go, leaving Cassie.

For a minute Cassie didn't say anything. He watched her smooth a loose thread in the fabric of her dress. Then she looked up and met his gaze.

"What are you going to do?" she asked.

He swallowed painfully. "We'll have to go to town after them."

Worry creased her smooth forehead. "Does it have to be that way?"

"Yes."

"Can't you—couldn't we talk to them?"

Anger flushed his face. "You didn't hang from that rope."

Her hand shot to her throat involuntarily. She went pale and her eyes glowed from colorless skin.

"I'm sorry," Phil said digustedly.

She looked down. "I don't know why I care," she said in a faint, strange-sounding little voice.

"You should want us to go," he said. "After Lester."

She raised her head. She didn't say anything. He thought she was going to cry. She simply stared at him, her great, luminous eyes going inside him.

The instant lasted. Their eyes locked together. Her lips parted, but she did not speak. Sluggish excitement thrummed in Phil's brain. Suddenly despite everything—the way he felt and knew he looked—he wanted her. It was impossible for his body to want her totally, but a void opened up inside him and he hurt vacantly, far more deeply and truly than the mob had hurt him, and he needed her. He saw the light in her hair and the slim lines of her legs beneath the smooth fabric of her dress, and the softness of her lips. Something—a fragile longing in her face—made him think she wanted him too.

He wanted to tell her. The words rose to his lips. His hands and arms tingled with the way she would feel in his arms. His torn mouth ached to feel her lips against it. All the aloneness of his life came onto him in a split-second and he saw how it might have been—how they might have been together, with laughter. His breath was shallow and uneven. He struggled within himself for the words.

The right words—the right gesture—and she would come to him.

On the porch, Sullivan said something to one of the men. The man answered.

Cassie looked suddenly away.

The moment was over. Phil looked down at his white, dirt-scarred right hand.

You've killed too many, he thought. You have to kill more.

That was what she had seen too. The killer.

He realized suddenly that he had never really thought of himself as a killer, the gunman that he was. He had known he was good with a gun. His way of living and thinking had been built around constant awareness, being alone and feared and hated, the bravado and quiet arrogance of the gunslinger.

He had always been Phil Patterson, Redwater, and he had always been going back to Redwater to make up for it someday, and have Cassie again, and be like he had once been. There had always been the lurking dream—the farm or ranch, the people respecting you, not wearing a gun, the kids running to you as you came in from a hard ride after cattle.

Now all at once he felt like the Patterson he had become. What a fool he had been to think he could be anything else! A killer. A gun. A man in the street with a holster slung low and big, soft hands and nothing inside but hate. A death machine. Nothing else.

He said huskily, "If Sullivan's through out there—"

Cassie rose quickly. "Yes," she said very softly. "I'll get him."

They didn't have to wait long for Killian to act.

It was less than an hour later that the men outside sprang up to their guns and Sullivan turned to look quickly out the door. From his cot Phil could see a lone rider coming from the blackjack woods and toward Janakowski, alone on a horse at the midpoint between woods and the house.

"Who is it?" Phil demanded, raising himself to an elbow.

"Can't see," Sullivan muttered, squinting through his hands.

Phil pulled himself to a sitting position. He reeled, then steadied himself to stare out onto the gray clearing.

The rider sat straight in the saddle. He held his hands high, clearly away from the gun at his belt or the rifle in the saddle scabbard. His gray hat was tilted back from his face.

"Grove," Phil muttered.

Sullivan turned to the door. "We'll blast that—"

"No!" Phil clipped.

Sullivan turned, his face a question.

"Let him come," Phil said thickly.

"What if he—"

"If he wants to talk, keep him on his horse. We can talk from here."

Sullivan frowned, obviously against it. But he opened the screen door and bawled, "Let 'im come up!" Then, in a lower tone to the men on the porch, "If the bastard makes a move, let 'im have it."

He let the screen close and came back beside Phil. "What the hell's he up to?"

Phil reached up and slipped Sullivan's gun from his belt.

Grove rode closer, going slow. His horse, a bay, picked its way almost gently. Thunder rocked over the cliff and echoed far down the valley. One of the men on the porch worked the bolt of his rifle and a slug hit the floor of the porch as the mechanism moved with a soft ratcheting sound.

Grove's keen, mild eyes glanced over the men on the porch as he reined up a dozen paces from the steps. He was wearing denims and a faded yellow shirt with torn elbows. A star gleamed dully on the shirt front.

"Patterson here?" he asked softly.

No one said anything.

"Ah'm looking for him," Grove said in the same tone.

"I'm here," Phil called.

Grove's eyes went to the door. Phil couldn't tell if he could see inside or not. His look was blank-eyed, groping. But he didn't show any surprise.

"Yur aw right," he said with his slow, disarming smile.

"What's on your mind?" Phil countered.

"Ah come for yuh, Phil."

Anger trickled into Phil's veins. He didn't say anything. Sullivan glared and cast around for another gun.

Grove's soft voice drawled, "We're right proud yuh got saved from thet lynchin' bunch, but yur still under arrest for killin' Lester."

"He didn't kill Lester, you moth-eaten bastard!" Sullivan roared.

"Cut it!" Phil hissed.

Grove grinned broadly. "Mebbe not, Mister whoever-you-are. But we gotta have a nice trial, legal."

Sullivan's knuckles cracked as he squeezed his hands together in fury.

Phil called back, "I'm not going, Grove." His body had cooled to nerveless readiness. The unfamiliar gun felt good in his hand.

Grove looked around at the men with rifles. "Guess ah can't force yuh, Phil, right now."

"I'll be in," Phil rapped.

"Right soon?" Grove asked lazily.

"Soon," Phil gritted.

"Thet's fine," Grove smiled. "Cause, see, they's some folks in there kind of upset 'bout Lester, 'n all. They're sayin' they better come see if they c'n *git* yuh."

Sullivan stalked to the door. "You come on out!" he rasped. "You bring your boys out and we'll see."

Grove smiled again. "Well, sir, yuh know thet could get real messy. We could have us a real war."

Phil's arms and legs went cold.

He saw clearly what decision Grove and Killian were giving him: Come into town and have it out, or get ready for what could develop into nearly a war. A fight that would involve almost everyone in the valley—these men and their families, maybe their hired hands if it got bloody—the people in town, Killian's gang. Killian wasn't leaving. He wasn't quitting. He had enough people in town blinded, despite the water rates, to build up a big group of men hot for Lester's murderer's blood.

Grove called laconically, "Yuh comin', Phil?"

"You'd better git!" Sullivan roared.

"Shut up," Phil snapped at him.

Sullivan turned, surprise etched on his rough features.

Grove waited, relaxed, confident.

"You ain't goin'," Sullivan muttered.

Phil looked at the gun in his hand. He could go and face them, or get every man here endangered, maybe killed, at the hands of their own kind. Killian held trumps. He could split the valley.

"Phil?" Grove called mildly.

Phil looked through the window at the face of one of the men holding a rifle. It was the retired farmer, Garner. His lean, weather-beaten face showed no fear. He was old, 70 maybe, and his teeth were gone, most of his hair, too, and he was skinny and mottle-skinned with age. But his jaws worked rhythmically on a chunk of tobacco. He showed no fear.

It was, Phil thought suddenly, their fight, after all. He was hired to do it. He wasn't a part of it. Why shouldn't they fight it, even if it meant a war through the whole valley?

But it wasn't that simple. They had hired him to do it. They had hired him because they weren't fighters and he was a fighter and they thought he could do the job.

If he didn't do it, he could never be here after it was over, no matter who won. He would be the mercenary who failed and rode on.

Grove rolled a cigarette and lit it. He flipped the match carelessly to the grass. He puffed smoke easily and looked at the darkening sky.

"Gonna come up a storm," he drawled. "Ah gotta get back."

Phil lurched to his feet. He didn't know what he would do.

But then, as he stood, pain racked his body. Ruptured membranes in his stomach stretched and seemed to tear further. He reeled dizzily.

"What're yuh gonna do, Phil?" Grove's voice called.

Phil staggered to the door. Anger burned through him. He shoved the screen open and limped onto the porch. The movement popped his shoulder open and he felt hot blood trickle down inside the tight bandage.

Grove looked at him without changing expression. "They beat yuh up a mite."

"Tell Killian," Phil said softly, enjoying the taste of the words, "that he won't need his deputies. I'll be in town before noon."

Chapter 14

"YOU'RE LOCO!" Sullivan raved. "You're so crazy in the head you don't know what you're doin'!"

Grove had ridden away, and Phil clumsily buttoned his shirt and tucked it in his trousers. He felt giddy and weak, and he was glad Cassie was still gone to the barn.

"Don't sweat about it," he said softly.

"You can't go in there plumb by yourself," Sullivan pleaded. "They'll pot you from a roof afore you get past the well."

"Maybe they will," Phil said, buckling on his gunbelt. "Maybe they'll want to do it right. Maybe Grove and Brewster will try to take me in the street, so everyone can see I got shot down fair and square."

"They won't do that," Sullivan muttered, pacing back and forth. "They'll plunk you with a rifle from the bank buildin'."

Phil worked the fingers of his right hand. "I'm betting they won't. They don't think I can take Grove and Brewster at once. If they shoot me down and everyone sees they did it trying to arrest me, Grove will be in as sheriff permanently. And I'll be out of the way just as long."

He examined Sullivan's gun, a crusty old war

model, and slipped it loosely into the well-oiled holster.

Sullivan stopped pacing and faced him squarely. His eyes looked wild and angry. "We're goin' with you!"

"No you're not," Phil clipped.

"We're goin'," Sullivan repeated stubbornly. "It's our town. You can't handle them guys by yourself."

Phil stared at him coldly. "Brewster and Grove?—I can handle them."

Sullivan strode to the door. "Boys?—Get in here!"

The men filed in, carrying their guns. They stared wide-eyed at Phil dressed and wearing a gun.

"Yuh ain't well," Garner muttered.

Phil worked his stiff hands again. He didn't answer.

"Boys," Sullivan said heavily, "Phil's goin' in after 'em by himself."

The five of them, Garner, Janakowski, O'Malley, Bryan and Eberhart, were all visibly shocked at the announcement.

"Aw no," Bryan, the youngest, murmured.

"We go too," Janakowski blurted.

Phil faced them. Weakness ebbed and flowed through him. His mouth was bleeding inside again.

"I can't talk plain with this mouth," he said. "I'm going."

Bryan started for the door. "I'll get the horses."

"No!" Phil snapped. He stared at them, struggling for words. "This is mine.—Don't you see this is my fight?—I'm the one they strung up. I'm the one that let Jake Michaels die. Maybe if I hadn't messed things up Lester would be alive too. I've—got—to go."

Bryan's Adam's apple bobbed up and down. "Phil—I wasn't here when the old sheriff got it, but—"

"I was," Garner said in his reed-like voice. "I knowed Michaels all his life. He din't die because Phil Patterson let 'im."

Phil shook his head. He couldn't let emotion—the soft kind—get in the way now.

He strode to the door.

"We're comin' with you," Sullivan said.

"Let me do it!" Phil hissed fiercely.

They recoiled from the burst. He stared at them for a moment, seeing in them friends.

He didn't think he could win. He hoped they sent Brewster and Grove out first, because hatred was gnawing at his insides and he wanted a chance at Brewster especially. He would go for Brewster first, and if Grove killed him he would at least have gotten Brewster first. That would be something.

Maybe, if Brewster was killed, Sullivan and the others would have a chance. Once the Phil Patterson thing was settled, the fight against Killian could be on the right plane again, not like a battle against the law.

He turned toward the barn and saw Cassie.

She saw him at the same time and stopped dead, her hand going to her mouth. Then she ran toward him.

"Phil!" she cried.

He caught her. She ran into his arms and stared up at him fearfully.

"I'm on my way to town, Cassie," he said, suddenly choked up.

Her huge eyes scanned his face and went glazed. "No!"

He looked past her toward the corral. "Which is your best horse?"

She seized his arms. "You're not going in there to be killed!"

He pushed her away and started forward.

"No!" she cried, dragging at him. "They'll kill you!"

He kept going.

"You're the only one *left*," she sobbed desperately.

The way she cried it stopped him. He turned and looked at her.

She stood bent-over, crying, her face in her hands.

"What do you mean?" he asked huskily.

"I'm supposed to be modest," she wept. "I'm not supposed to—to—" She fumbled, raising her face. "I'm not supposed to love you!" she cried bitterly.

Phil rocked back. He didn't say anything. He didn't move. Cassie stood facing him, the tears streaming down her face. Her eyes blazed with the emotion he now recognized, now, stunned and amazed, knew clearly.

"You—love—me?" he choked.

"I do," she replied in a burst. "I shouldn't say it but I do—and if you go in there and get killed—"

He ran to her and she came into his arms. Her face buried itself against his chest and she was crying bitterly, almost without control or resistance, the broken sobs of all her losses. He held her close, unmoving, and the fragrance of her hair was the stuff of dreams. Her firm young body pressed against him, shaken by sobs, and her hands had stolen around his neck.

"Cassie," he muttered in confusion. "I didn't think—"

Her face came up, large and blurred-near, streaked with tears. Her lips quavered. "You came back—I didn't think it would make any difference only it has—maybe not for you—I know being a widow—it's too soon and I shouldn't, Phil—I know it isn't right for me because I was wrong about you when daddy—when that happened—I hated you, I thought I did—but it's the same—"

Phil's insides burst with joy. He wanted to shout. She was close against him in his arms and he still couldn't wholly comprehend it. She loved him! Who could he tell? He thought of Jonathon. He wanted to tell Jonathon, and take Cassie to his mother and let her know too. The dream could be. He could make up for everything. He could be with Cassie.

Cassie sobbed, "Please don't go to town."

For an instant he had almost forgotten. Her words dashed icy water into his veins.

There were still Killian and Grove and Brewster —the others too—in Redwater. There were still those who wanted him to hang. There was still Lester's murder to pay back, and his own innocence to prove, and the debt to be paid to everybody.

He tried to disengage himself from Cassie.

"No!" she whispered.

"I have to," he muttered doggedly.

"You don't! Let them do it!"

He shook his head and stepped back from her. He ached to take her back into his arms, but he stood fast. "I can't let them do it. They hired me. You think if I let them do it those people in town will ever believe I didn't kill Lester? Not all of them."

"We don't care," Cassie pleaded.

"We have to," he bit out. "This isn't just getting Killian because it's a job, or because they tried to hang me. It's something I have to do. Can you understand? I have to do it. I have to do something right for—for everybody—for Redwater."

"You owe the place you live something," he said slowly. "You have to be worthy of it. You have to show what you are."

She stepped toward him, her face convulsed with fear. "Please, Phil—"

"I'm going," he rapped.

"They'll—" Her voice broke. "They'll kill you."

Phil swayed. He didn't really want to go in. He thought how much easier it would be to lead the men in and rush Killian in a group, gang the others and take over. But that wasn't really the way he wanted it—the way it had to be.

He looked at Cassie, saw the torn longing in her eyes, the tears streaking her face, her anguished, knotted hands. His arms and legs hurt already from the beating he had taken. He told himself that he couldn't stand a ride to town—he wasn't ready—

Cassie raised a supplicating hand toward him.

He turned. "I'm going," he choked. "Wait."

He rode alone across the red clay of the creek bottom, and guided the horse up the rise that overlooked the town. The ride had shaken his wounds, and his legs burned with pain. His head throbbed. The hiss of his blood in his ears made him feel detached and unreal. Only the roar of hail in the boiling black clouds overhead kept him from feeling totally cut off from his surroundings.

Mentally he was alert. He had gone over the possibilities. The only way Killian could discredit the ones who had hired him was by having him arrested and tried for Lester's murder. Killian could select the jury before the judge came, and maybe he even had his own judge. It would be far better than shooting from a roof-top or letting another lynch mob form—if in daylight, after a failure, a lynch mob could be formed.

But there was always the possibility of the unanticipated. Phil had tried to go over all the possibilities as he rode. He felt no nervousness, just a taut readiness. He had to get it over fast, no matter what they did. He knew Sullivan and the others would be saddling up right now, as soon as they were sure he was out of sight, and getting ready to follow him. If they weren't to get into it, and maybe get hurt or killed, he had to settle it fast, or do his best.

His horse topped the rise, and cool wind swirled into his face. After the sultry stillness of the valley it was a cold shock. But in the next instant the wind turned hot and humid again, and he glanced up at the ruddy-colored clouds. There would be a bad storm. But this wasn't a time when the clouds interested him. He looked down into the town.

Clearly everyone knew he was coming. The street was deserted. Only a few horses stood at the hitching rails. A single wagon stood empty near one of the stores. Trees bent back in the wind and dust blew up to obscure everything. He tasted the grit of the air as he clucked to his horse and started down toward the town.

At the bottom of the hill he let the horse walk. He loosened his gun in its holster. It was a good gun, but he wished he had his own. The butt on this one was a shade shorter and thicker. He had noticed that as he slowly drew the gun a few times to loosen his sore stiff fingers.

Now he let the gun rest in the holster. He held his right hand near his waist, holding the reins with his left hand. The wind, cold again, pressed his shirt against his chest. The broad brim of his hat flapped back and dust blew into his face. His eyes squinted through the gale at the roof-tops of the first buildings. It was difficult to see. He could see no one.

Lightning crackled bitterly and a blinding flash bolted down to his left, into a rolling pasture behind a single cottonwood. Simultaneously the sky burst apart in a deafening thunderclap that made his horse jump and pick up his pace, ears laid back, eyes rolling nervously.

Leaning into the wind, Phil let the horse go. The first house was just ahead—now beside him—and nothing happened. Tar paper on the roof flapped in the gale. Papers plastered themselves against the fence around the yard. Dust grayed the air and other houses loomed up like ghosts ahead. The storm was building directly over head. Phil rode past the first store, a feed store that was closed tight and apparently deserted.

His nerves had tightened. He scanned the dust-blown confusion of the sidewalks. He saw no one. The storm roared deafeningly. No rain yet. A canvas door flap whipped back in the wind, the horse moved on stolidly now, beaten by the storm, moving slowly.

Ahead Phil saw the rounded curve in the street, and the garish front of the Golden Eagle. He saw light through the front windows. They would be there. None of the upstairs windows were open, and a glance showed nothing about either of the banks. The hotel, beaten-down and shoddy-looking with its yellow and brown paint in the gray light of the storm, stared vacantly with empty windows.

Phil guided his horse to the side of the street. His pelvis shot pain as he swung down. He checked his gun. He flipped the reins over the hitching rail and turned toward the street, and the curve some seventy-five paces distant, where the saloon faced down toward him.

His feet dragged in the heavy dust as he started forward. Grit in his mouth cut into the aching holes where teeth had been broken out. It was hard to breathe; his lungs spasmed near coughing and he fought not to cough, to be alert and not miss a thing. The back of his neck prickled with the sensation of being watched. He wanted to turn and see if anyone was on a roof behind him, but he resisted. The bravado—the turning of your back—had always won. They wouldn't shoot him in the back. He thought they wouldn't because it would look bad before the town; but some other way, with the extra sense he had developed to maintain his life, he knew.

The fresh, cold smell of rain hit him in the face, and thunder boomed overhead. A torn and dirty newspaper scuffled along the street and wrapped itself around his legs. He kicked it free without missing stride. He clenched and unclenched his right hand, twinges shooting up into his elbow. Still the door of the Golden Eagle remained closed. Would he have to go in to them?

The gun moved heavy against his thigh. He hadn't had enough practice in the last few days. He hadn't had a good practice since riding in with Jonathon. He felt ready. He felt good. This was what he understood. He remembered the time in Dodge and Laredo, and the other times, and this was familiar. His eyes stayed on the door of the saloon. They couldn't bushwhack him now. His challenge was clear to every man in town. It had to be met.

Another dozen paces, and the bank was at his right and the hotel loomed up in a pall of dust at his left. He saw in the edge of his vision that there were faces at windows—strained, intent men's faces, watching. He kept moving forward, walking slowly.

Then the door of the saloon opened.

For a moment it swung open, and he saw no one. He saw inside, and figures moved back in the light. Then a figure moved into the door, and stepped outside slowly, onto the porch. The man's gun was tied down low and he wore no hat. His blond hair whipped in the wind. His yellow shirt sleeves were rolled up past the elbow. His hands hung loose and relaxed. Grove.

Grove stepped sideways in an easy motion, his shoulders level and his head turned toward Phil. Another figure darkened the door and came out. Brewster, a blue vest buttoned over his thin chest, his long arms dangling, walked straight out the door and across the porch to the steps. He stepped down with his right foot, then with his left, and into the yellow dust of the street. He didn't pause. He started walking.

Phil kept his eyes on Brewster. He saw Grove at the same time. Grove walked easily along the walk to his right, coming toward the corner opposite the bank. Divided, Brewster in the middle, Grove off to the right. Phil couldn't expect to get both of them.

Thunder rolled across the sky. It was intensely dark, but Phil saw every detail. Brewster was unshaven, and his eyes, even at thirty paces, were alive and glittering. A slight smile of anticipation split his thin lips. On the front of his vest he wore a small star of a deputy. He walked slightly bent to the left so that his right hand was just below holster, bent outward.

Grove moved past the front of the barber shop at a pace equal to Brewster's. Grove was perhaps ten paces farther away than Brewster now, but he could close that gap in one bound. His face showed no emotion whatsoever. He watched Phil intently, the way a man would watch a card game in which he had no stake.

Phil stopped.

Brewster kept coming, perhaps a shade slower. His expression had not changed. His gun was tied down with a fresh leather thong. The loose end of it flapped against his leg. His spurs cut tiny trails in the dust as he took a step.

Grove gently moved down the steps of the sidewalk and sidled into the street at Phil's right. His hand was higher now, beginning to tense.

Phil felt nothing. His entire being focused on their movements. Brewster stopped walking. Phil faced Brewster. He could just see Grove out of the corner of his eye. Brewster grinned and a string of saliva ran down his chin. His hand quivered.

Thunder crashed.

Brewster fell to the side.

It meant draw. Phil's hand shot to his holster and the gun came out clean. His thumb hit the trigger on the way up and the gun roared. Brewster's gun had just cleared leather when Phil's bullet hit him in the shoulder or arm, spinning him. His gun went off wildly and leaped out of his hand. He reeled and started to fall.

Phil whirled in a crouch. Grove's gun spat. A puff of smoke touched Phil's leg and suddenly he was down on his side. His gun went off and Grove lurched forward, doubling over. Shots echoed across the street. Phil fired again. Grove fell forward and hit on top of his head like a kid doing a somersault. Then he fell sideways. His legs twitched.

Phil spun back toward Brewster. Brewster had come to his feet. He lunged for the gun in the dusty street. Phil thumbed the hammer.

The hammer fell on a dead shell.

Brewster got the gun and turned, his face contorted with hate and pain. His gun came up.

Phil desperately thumbed the hammer again. The cylinder turned and the hammer fell and the gun rocked back in his hand.

Brewster shot over backward and sprawled limp. The gun fell from his hand.

Phil limped forward. His leg was burning up. He had caught a bullet in the fleshy part of the calf, a graze. He felt weak. He looked down at Brewster.

The egg-white eyes of death stared back at him. A bluish hole fringed with crimson was directly in the middle of Brewster's forehead.

Then Brewster's body jumped and the spang of a carbine lanced across the street.

Phil leaped for the sidewalk. Someone was on top. The carbine slammed again and the bullet puffed dust at his side. He dove hard and hit the boards of the sidewalk. His chest exploded in pain with the impact of falling, and he rolled wildly, hitting against the front of a store. He came to a knee and scanned the buildings across the street. He couldn't see anyone. The bodies of Grove and Brewster lay where they had fallen. The first drops of rain spatted down onto the dusty street.

Then, in the instant, the sky opened up. A brilliant blue burst of lightning ripped the length of the street and the rain roared down. The street was immediately soaked, and rain pounded into quick puddles. Cold air gushed across the sidewalk. Phil looked over the still-hot barrel of his gun. The buildings across the street blurred and all but vanished. The storm rumbled and raged, icy sheets of water tearing down and splattering onto the boards on which he knelt.

Shivering, Phil glanced up and down the sidewalk. The open door of the Golden Eagle was twenty feet away. He came to his feet and pounded forward toward it. His mind raced, calculating as he ran. One on a roof, two down. Schwartz or Baxon on the roof. That left Killian and Tub and the odd one.

At that moment Baxon stepped into the doorway of the saloon. He had a rifle at his hip. Phil's gun was in position and he snapped a shot. Baxon's rifle tipped up and went off and he opened his mouth—maybe he shouted, Phil could never know—and went backward. The rifle fell.

Phil burst into the doorway. His shoulder slammed the back-swinging door. Baxon lay flat, his arms crooked in death. The place was jammed with men. It was hot and smoky. Tub, hulking but amazingly agile, leaped from nowhere.

Phil couldn't dodge. His wet boots slipped on the wood floor. He went over on his side under the avalanche of Tub's weight. A fist dug to his body and he hit the floor, losing the gun. The rough material of Tub's shirt gouged across his face and something hit him.

For a moment he thought he had gotten free.

Then he realized he had lost control of his body.

Then he realized—

Nothing.

Chapter 15

PHIL CAME TO all at once. He opened his eyes with a sudden shock, and saw Sullivan and the others standing in a line over him, guns at a level.

They had their guns leveled on the men in the bar. Standing in the front of the mob were Tub, his right hand dripping blood, and Killian. Killian was untouched, seemingly as cool and detached as ever, a cigar in his immaculate right hand. He was staring arrogantly at Sullivan.

"He's a murderer," he said evenly. "You men cannot take the law into your own hands."

"You just shut up or I'll splatter you all over that wall," Sullivan glowered, waving his gun menacingly.

One of the others said, "Hey, Phil's awake."

Sullivan, his hair on end, looked down quickly.

Phil struggled to a sitting position. His leg was numb and he couldn't get up.

"Set tight," Sullivan muttered with rough gentleness. "This big bastard really tapped you."

Phil touched the side of his head and felt a new lump. He was still dizzy. His mouth was bleeding again. He was almost used to it. He hurt all over. There had been shooting. Blue smoke hung in the air and the smell of the powder burned his nostrils.

The men standing behind Killian were lax-mouthed and surprised. Tub stood stoop-shouldered, blinking, repeatedly glancing at Killian as if for orders. The men around Sullivan dripped water in puddles at their feet. Their faces were white and drawn. Each had his finger on the trigger of a revolver or rifle. Bryan held an ancient shotgun, a double-barrel .12 gauge bird gun. It had fancy scroll work on the housing, but it was rusty.

Killian said smoothly, "You men have no right to come here and interfere. You may be citizens. That doesn't change the fact that his man killed Lester Michaels. And now he has killed three others."

He gestured toward the door, and Phil saw that they had brought in the bodies of Brewster and Grove. They were laid beside Baxon. A rivulet of dried blood stained the floor beside the bodies.

Sullivan muttered, "Phil didn't kill anybody that didn't need it real bad. That don't include Lester because he didn't kill Lester."

Some of the men behind Killian murmured and moved nervously.

One of them, a sunburned cowboy with skinned hands and long, gawky legs, cleared his throat. "They found Michaels' carcass in this guy's room."

Some of the others muttered agreement.

"Yeah!" Sullivan bawled angrily. "An' Killian's stooges put 'im there!"

Killian turned the cigar in his fingers. "Charges like that only show your recklessness. It is clear that this hired killer—"

"Cut it!" Sullivan roared angrily.

Killian took a step forward. "This man must go to jail."

"You move," Sullivan gritted, "and I let you have it."

Killian stopped. He turned in an aside to the others. "I plan to write the U. S. Marshal. I shall want some of you as witnesses when he arrives."

"You're not gonna write anybody," Sullivan said. "You're gonna be in that jail your own self."

Killian smiled. "On what charge?"

"On what charge!" Sullivan rumbled incredulously.

Phil saw sweat on Killian's dark forehead, but it was the only sign that the man was under pressure. "Yes. What charge will you lodge against me? I asked some of my men to arrest this killer, and he killed them. Does that make me a wanted man?"

"How about Schwartz?" Bryan asked in his nasal voice. "He powdered us with lead when we rode in."

Killian shrugged. "I cannot be responsible when a man gets drunk."

"He also got bored," Sullivan said darkly. "And that's about what's gonna happen to you."

"You can't," Killian said sharply.

Sullivan took a shambling step forward.

"Hold it," Phil rapped.

Sullivan looked at him.

"He's right," Phil said. "We don't have a thing on him."

Killian again smiled. "Help from a condemned murderer."

Phil ignored it. Dull anger boiled within him. He looked at Sullivan and the others. "We can't prove anything at all."

"But my lord!" Sullivan stammered. "He's—I mean the water!"

"It's his water," Phil said bitterly.

Sullivan's shoulders dropped.

Killian turned to the crowd. "Will you men who can write please see the bartender and sign to be witnesses?—I—"

"That won't be necessary," Phil snapped.

Killian turned.

Phil climbed to his feet. He swayed dizzily and might have fallen if somebody hadn't grabbed his arm. He sucked in a deep breath and got his balance, staring at Killian through a shower of yellow stars.

"You won't have to sign witnesses," he muttered. He looked at Sullivan. "Give me a gun."

Killian blanched as Sullivan handed Phil a pearl-handled .44.

"What do you plan to do?" Killian asked, his voice a trifle higher pitched.

Phil balanced the gun in his hand. "Is this loaded?"

"Yeah," Sullivan grunted, puzzled.

"What do you plan to do?" Killian repeated.

Phil faced him. "Maybe if we let this go, you'll get a Marshal in here and I'll hang. Right now we can't prove anything about you. You don't have anything on us, not even me. I don't know if what you say will stand up in a real court or not."

He paused and took a breath. "It doesn't make any difference."

Killian backed up a half a pace. His cigar dropped from his fingers.

"You've got them poisoned," Phil gritted. "I could live here a hundred years and some of them would still say I shot Lester."

Killian mustered bravado. "You shouldn't have done—"

"Don't bother," Phil said very softly. The room

was absolutely quiet. He leveled the gun on Killian's chest. "I'm a hired killer. You're right about that. I came here to kill you. Sullivan can't. He's got family. I can. I've done it before. I can get out. I'm going to enjoy it."

"Now wait," Killian said hoarsely. His composure started to break.

"I didn't kill Lester," Phil grated. "But that won't help you."

Sullivan said, "Phil—"

"Shut up," Phil clipped. "It's my business."

Sweat trickled down Killian's face. Suddenly he looked shrunken. He trembled. He looked imploringly at the ox-like Tub, then back into the muzzle of Phil's gun. The men behind Killian shoved at each other and magically got out from behind him. The mirror behind the bar reflected vacantly behind him. His eyes widened and rolled. Phil slipped his finger over the trigger of the gun.

"Look here," Killian whispered harshly. His voice had gone. "Look here, Patterson. The evidence about Lester—it's not proof—if you say you didn't do it—"

"What I say doesn't matter," Phil gritted. He took a step nearer.

"But I think we may have been hasty," Killian said, words falling out over each other. "Maybe you're innocent. Maybe we shouldn't press charges at all." He turned to the men around him. "Hear that, boys? I think we've made a mistake. I think perhaps Mister Patterson didn't kill Michaels."

Phil stepped still closer, three feet away. "I'm going to gut-shoot you," he said softly. "It takes a long time to die that way. I'll shoot real low. Maybe you'll bleed a whole day."

Killian made a sick sound in his throat. His

hands went to his stomach. His chin wobbled. Terror imprinted itself on his features. He looked around wildly.

"You can't let this maniac shoot me," he stammered. "He's a killer! He enjoys it!—You can't—"

"Shut up," Phil said so softly that it cracked like a whip in the silent room.

No one moved. Killian's teeth chattered. His cheeks turned ashen. His body crumpled inside the stiff finery of his suit.

"Ever been shot?" Phil asked conversationally. "In the stomach is the worst place. They can't fix it. You bleed inside. You fill up inside with blood. You get black under the skin and there's nothing you can do about the way it hurts. I knew a man shot himself in the head. He crawled all the way across a town to get a gun and kill himself so the pain wouldn't last any more."

"No," Killian sobbed. "No.—I'll leave!" He brightened with hope. "Look here, Patterson! I'll leave Redwater. I won't press charges. I won't do anything. I'll leave right now." He spun around. "Does anyone have a horse I can buy?—I'll pay anything." He turned back to Phil. "I'll leave right now. In the storm. I don't care—"

Phil cocked the gun's hammer back. "It isn't enough."

Killian's eyes rolled. His hands clutched together. His face was gleaming wet with perspiration. Saliva dribbled down his chin. *"Please,"* he whispered. "I'm not asking anything."

Phil lowered the gun so that it pointed at Killian's stomach. "Ready?"

Killian swung around. "Tub killed Lester!" he cried shrilly.

Tub lurched as if he had been hit. Men exclaimed hoarsely.

"Yes!" Killian sobbed, almost laughing hysterically. "Tub did it—I didn't know anything about it! I heard about it just a little while ago and I didn't know what to do! He's a killer! He's killed others! He's crazy! You didn't do it, Patterson, Tub did it, I know that now! Let me tell—"

Tub's great body lurched forward. With a throaty roar he jumped at Killian.

Killian tried to dodge. Someone's gun went off deafeningly and Tub straightned up rigid, his great body straining, his eyes wide. His big, stupid face looked shocked and hurt.

But it was for only an instant. His shirt blotched crimson, and his hands dragged out to the bar. A dozen bottles shattered and smashed off the counter to the floor. One of the bottles came up in Tub's hand.

Killian cried out and threw up his arms, but it didn't help.

Tub's huge body swung in a tremendous uncoiling motion.

The bottle disintegrated in Killian's face, glass ripping him to shreds. The impact shot over the room like the breaking of a ripe melon.

Then, before anyone could move, Killian fell.

Tub stood there for another split-second, death written on his face. His eyes glazed. The bloody fragments of the bottle fell from his hand.

He toppled slowly, life quitting his huge body slowly. He fell onto Killian with a plopping noise. Phil looked down.

Tub's massive body didn't cover Killian's face. Killian, too, was dead.

Chapter 16

THE RAIN stopped during the night, and the next morning the sun shone down on soaked pastureland. The town of Redwater lay in a sea of the ugliest, most beautiful mud anyone in the valley had ever seen.

"The drouth's over," Jonathon said exultantly. "The drouth's over and we got all the water we want!"

"Well," Phil said slowly, for his mouth was caked over and he wanted it to heal, "our problems aren't over."

Jonathon frowned. "Yeah. All them cows are still out there someplace."

"Maybe we can find them," Phil said.

Jonathon grinned broadly and wiped his grimy face with the back of his hand. "You already done a good day's work, brother."

Phil stared at the ceiling, where a leak in the roof had let water in to stain the wallpaper. "I didn't know if he'd crack."

"I wisht I'd *been* there," Jonathon moaned. "It must've been great!"

Phil remembered it. "It wasn't great or anything like it. For a minute there I was really going to let him have it."

Jonathon beamed. "Well, you din't haf to. Now all you gotta do is get well so you can get your badge on an'—"

"No badge for me," Phil said quickly.

Jonathon stared at him. "Ever'body in town's talkin' about it, Phil. They're countin' on you. They're a hunderd percent behind you now, boy. You should hear 'em!"

Phil raised his right hand to look at it. "No more," he said simply.

"Aw Phil!" Jonathon remonstrated disgustedly.

"I'm going to be a farmer," Phil said softly, liking the way it sounded. "Or maybe some cattle. I don't know."

"Heck," Jonathon said. "When you get back on your feet you'll feel diffrent."

Phil smiled tiredly and didn't argue.

Bothered by his silence, Jonathon muttered, "I don't know why you wouldn't wanna be sheriff, an' put on your gun an' take care of things around here."

Phil still didn't say anything.

"Listen!" Jonathon prodded desperately. "Cassie's gonna be here any minute! Now let's get this settled before she does. Why don't you wanna put on that gun?"

Phil looked at him, and grinned. "You just gave the reason, Jonathon. Because Cassie's going to be here. She's going to be here for a long time."